# FUGITIVE X

## A **REVOLUTION** 19 NOVEL

### GREGG ROSENBLUM

HARPER TEEN

*An Imprint of HarperCollinsPublishers*

alloy**entertainment**

Produced by Alloy Entertainment
1700 Broadway, New York, NY 10019
www.alloyentertainment.com

Library of Congress Cataloging-in-Publication Data
Rosenblum, Gregg.
  Fugitive X : a Revolution 19 novel / Gregg Rosenblum. — First edition.
    pages  cm
  Sequel to: Revolution 19.
  Summary: "As a war between robots and humans looms on the horizon, Nick, Kevin, and
Cass continue to battle the bots that enslaved humanity—but when they are separated, they
must fight the war on their own"— Provided by publisher.
  ISBN 978-0-06-212599-6
  [1. Robots—Fiction. 2. Survival—Fiction. 3. Brothers and sisters—Fiction. 4. War—Fiction.
5. Science fiction.] I. Title.
PZ7.R7191763Fu 2014                                                    2013015446
[Fic]—dc23                                                                      CIP
                                                                                  AC

Typography by Liz Dresner

14 15 16 17 18   CG/RRDH   10 9 8 7 6 5 4 3 2 1

First paperback edition, 2015

"CASS, OPEN YOUR EYES!" NICK CRIED. HOW COULD SHE STILL BE ALIVE, with all that blood on the grass? "Cass!" he said again, but she didn't respond. His sister was dying. Bots were nearby.

The bots. Nick realized, with a wave of dizzy nausea, what he had to do. They were her only chance. He bent down and touched his forehead to her cheek, then whispered in her ear. "Don't die," he said, his voice choking. "Stay alive, and I'll come for you, I promise."

## BOOKS BY GREGG ROSENBLUM

*To Mac and Beatrice Menschel, and*
*Max and Gertrude Rosenblum, without whom I*
*(and therefore this book) wouldn't exist.*

# CHAPTER 1

NICK LED KEVIN AND CASS BACK TO WHERE THEY HAD STASHED THEIR packs outside the City. It seemed like a lifetime ago. He thought he'd need Cass to find the exact location, but he was the first to see the broken branches that marked the hiding spot. It was still incredible and strange, after all those years of blindness in one eye, to be able to see with such clarity.

Their packs were unopened and dry. Nick opened his pack and checked the contents. A bedroll. A spare pair of socks and underwear. A copy of an old-fashioned paper book, *Adventures of Huckleberry Finn*, that he had found in his family's emergency shelter. A sweater that his mother had knit for him, from their neighbor's sheep's wool. He brought the rough fabric up to his face. It smelled like dry leaves and campfire smoke—it still smelled like his Freepost, which no longer existed, thanks to the bots.

They shouldered their packs, then climbed back onto their scoots. The road this close to the City was in good enough shape for them to ride on. Soon, though, they found themselves slowing down more and more to weave through the cracks in the pavement and the brush and tree limbs and occasional burned-out vehicle scattered across the road.

Nick was thinking that it was almost time to ditch the scoots, and then Kevin nearly flipped over his handlebars hitting a rock, and that decided it. Nick climbed off his scoot, dumped it behind the rubble pile of a destroyed pre-Revolution building, and headed into the trees. Kevin and Cass followed close behind.

The trees were too thin to be a proper forest, especially with the road and pre-Rev buildings so nearby, but still, when Nick stepped off the road, feeling dirt and grass under his feet and surrounded by green, he took a deep breath and felt a small knot of tension in his stomach release. Without warning he felt tired, like he just needed to sit down. He stopped so abruptly in his tracks that Kevin stumbled into his back.

"Sorry," Nick said. He didn't move, gathering his strength. Kevin gave him an odd look and nudged him on the shoulder.

"Come on," Kevin said. "Keep moving. The bots are probably back online by now."

Nick winced, even from Kevin's soft push. He was still

hurting all over from the explosion in the mainframe room, and the ride out of the City on the rough road had made things even worse. Kevin was right, of course. They had to put some distance between themselves and the City. The mainframe backup would probably be running by now, which meant that the bots would be operational again—and coming after them.

As if on cue, an all-too-familiar hum rose from the south, filling his chest. "Down!" he said, hitting the ground and crawling to deeper cover. Kevin and Cass were on the ground just as quickly, scrambling for the trees.

The noise grew louder and louder. Nick rolled onto his back and watched the sky. The painful hum reached its peak as a warbird flew overhead, passing to the east of their hiding spot. He watched the black bot fade into a speck. Everything he had been through in the City—re-education, getting a bot eye, his mother not recognizing him, feeling certain he was about to die—it all struck him at once. He lay there, letting it all wash over him, then forced his racing emotions under control and pushed himself to his feet. Kevin and Cass were already standing, waiting for him.

"You okay?" asked Cass.

"Fine," said Nick. "Let's get farther from the road. Bots are obviously back online. We're going to have to find that Freepost to the north to meet up with Lexi and Farryn. . . . We can't wait for them on the road anymore."

Cass frowned, then nodded. She had to be thinking the

same thing, Nick knew. There were so many ifs . . . *if* Doc was able to safely get their chips out . . . *if* they escaped the City in time . . . *if* they made it far enough to get to forest thick enough to shield them . . . *if* they managed to survive in the woods when they had lived their entire lives in the City . . . *if* they were able to find this northern Freepost. It was going to be a miracle if they saw Lexi and Farryn again. Cass took the lead, followed by Kevin. Nick sighed and began walking after his brother and sister. The only good thing about being bruised and cut all over was that he couldn't pick any one spot to focus on. When everything hurt, it all sort of canceled itself out, as long as you didn't think about it too much, or get shoved on the shoulder by your little brother.

They walked in silence, pushing occasionally west into better cover as they continued mostly north. Nick was happy to let Cass lead—she knew what she was doing in the forest. They all did, of course—they had been hiking through woods pretty much their entire lives. They moved almost without sound, picking their way carefully through the undergrowth without thinking about it. Even Kevin, who at the Freepost had complained his way through every forestry hike, moved quietly.

The only problem with Cass breaking a trail was that she sometimes forgot that the people behind her weren't as small or athletic, and she'd set too aggressive a pace. But she was going slowly by her standards, which Nick realized with a bit of embarrassment was an unspoken concession to his beat-up state.

Cass froze, held her hand up, then dropped silently to the ground. Nick hit the dirt, his heart beating wildly. Ten feet ahead of him, Kevin also flung himself down, on a patch of grass.

"What is it?" asked Kevin. Cass shook her head angrily and put her hand over her mouth.

*Bots on the ground?* thought Nick. *Peteys? Sphere bots? Are we really going to be recaptured so quickly?* He was more angry than afraid. There was no way he was going back to re-education. No way he was going to let the bots take Cass or Kevin.

Cass was ten feet past Kevin, tucked under a bush at the crest of a small rise that they had been climbing. He desperately wanted to crawl to her, to see what they were facing, but she was holding her palm up, facing them, signaling *Wait. Don't move.* She was intently watching something down the far side of the slope. Finally, Cass glanced back at them and waved her hand toward her, then patted the ground. *Come, but slowly. And stay low.*

Nick crept along the ground toward Cass, moving as fast as possible without rustling the undergrowth. After what seemed like minutes but was probably only twenty seconds, he reached Kevin and Cass at the crest of the slope. Unconsciously holding his breath, he tucked himself under the bush next to his brother and sister and peered down the hill.

Fifty yards away, at the far end of a clearing, stood two men. Nick let his breath out in surprise and relief. "Humans," he whispered, realizing just how tensed he had been to see bots. The men wore camouflage gear and would have been difficult to see if they had been still. But they were pacing slowly up and down and speaking to each other, gesturing with their hands, their voices too low for Nick to make out what they were saying. They both had buzz-cut hair. One was heavily muscled, with a barrel chest, and the other was thin, with long arms and legs that made him seem much taller than the first man even though they were nearly the same height. Over their shoulders were slung long rifles, dull black barrels with scopes and small power supplies at the butt end.

"See the energy cells?" whispered Kevin, reading Nick's mind. "Energy bursters, or maybe just energy-propelled bullets, but definitely military gear."

"I know. Shut up," said Nick.

"Could probably knock down a tree with one shot, if they went full burst," said Kevin.

"Be quiet," scolded Cass.

"We should find out who they are," whispered Kevin. "They're not bots, after all."

Cass glared at Kevin and put her hand over his mouth. He slapped her hand away, rustling the bush. The thin man snapped his head in their direction, his rifle suddenly in his hands. Nick, Kevin, and Cass hunkered down deeper into the bush. The man took a step toward their hiding spot. His partner now had his rifle in his hands as well and was scanning the woods carefully, the muzzle sweeping the trees.

The thin man paused, listening, still facing the siblings' hiding spot. Nick stared down at the man and thought about what Kevin had said, that one full burst from the rifle would knock down a tree. Should he stand up, introduce himself, before being killed, mistaken for game? Kevin was right—these were humans, after all, not bots. But then he thought of the hermit with the knife they had confronted, what seemed like so long ago. And the true believers, back in the City. No, not all humans were allies. He lay still, putting a hand on the backs of both Cass and Kevin, ready to yank them to their feet and get them running if need be.

The thin man took another step toward their hiding spot, squinting, seeming to be looking right at them. Nick tensed and tightened his grip. The man paused for a long moment, his rifle aimed at their bush, before he finally let his rifle drop and slung it back over his shoulder. He shrugged at his partner, who also lowered his weapon. The big man nodded toward the woods, then headed into the trees to the west. The thin man glanced once more in their direction, then turned and followed, disappearing after a few moments.

Nick continued to lie still, his hands pushing down gently on the backs of Kevin and Cass to tell them not to get up. After a few seconds, Kevin rolled over, pushing Nick's hand away.

"You almost got us killed!" Kevin said.

"What are you talking about?" said Nick. "And keep your voice down. They may still be close."

"I mean," said Kevin, more quietly, "that we almost got mistaken for squirrels and shot for dinner." He stood up, brushing dirt off his shirt and pants. "They were people. In the forest. All we had to do was stand up and let them know we weren't squirrels or bots."

"What if they shot us anyway?" said Nick. "We have no idea who they were."

"They were people!" said Kevin. "With guns. Guns that could take down bots. They were probably a patrol from this Freepost we're trying to find, and they would have taken us right to it."

"Maybe," said Cass. "Maybe not. It wasn't safe. We don't know anything about them. We have to be careful."

"So now we're hiding from bots *and* people?" said Kevin.

"People with guns, yeah," said Nick.

Kevin shook his head in disgust and stomped off.

"Stay out of the clearing!" Nick called to Kevin's back. Kevin, about to step into the open space, hesitated, then pushed through the trees to the right, staying in tree cover, pushing branches angrily out of his way.

"Come on," said Cass to Nick. "We'd better catch up to him before he does something stupid."

# CHAPTER 2

THEY DIDN'T SEE ANY MORE BOTS, OR PEOPLE, THAT DAY. KEVIN trudged along in silence, brooding, ignoring Cass's occasional attempts at conversation. That night, while it was his turn to keep guard, Kevin watched his brother and sister sleeping, using their backpacks for pillows. His stomach growled; all he had eaten for dinner was a handful of sour berries. He tried to let his anger go. But he couldn't. He shifted his back against the tree he was sitting against, hoping to find a more comfortable position. He sat silently for a few more minutes, then noted the location of the moon in a clear patch of sky between a gap in the trees. "Late enough," he muttered to himself. He stood up, stretched, then walked over and nudged Nick with his foot. Nick grunted but didn't move, so Kevin nudged him a bit harder. Not quite a kick, although he was tempted. Nick rolled over and sat up, yawning. "My watch already?" he said.

"They must have been from the Freepost," Kevin said.

Nick stood up slowly. He looked confused for a moment, then shook his head, frowning. "You don't know that," he said. "And didn't we already have this conversation?"

"Those rifles weren't just for hunting game," Kevin said. "I bet they were trackers. All we had to do was stand up and we'd be sleeping in a shelter right now."

Nick shrugged and held his hands out at his sides, palms up. "Or we'd be dead," he said. "What do you know about them? Nothing. Except that they were holding burst rifles."

"They were people. Free. In the woods," said Kevin. "Like us."

Nick walked over to the same tree Kevin had used for his watch. He sat down and put his back against the trunk. "Look, kid, it's done. It was too risky. We'll find the Freepost on our own."

Kevin felt a rush of annoyance. "It's Kevin," he said. "Not kid. No more kid."

Nick shrugged. "Yeah, fine. Whatever. No more kid. Go to sleep."

"Don't tell me to go to sleep," said Kevin.

Nick chuckled. "Fine, then stay awake. But keep quiet at least. No point waking up Cass, or broadcasting to any bots or hunters exactly where we are."

"I'm awake," said Cass. She rolled over to face them. "And if there were any bots within a half mile of here they'd have heard you two idiots arguing. Will both of you shut up, please?"

"I was just saying . . ." began Kevin.

"Save it for the morning, Kevin," said Cass. "Right now I don't care."

Kevin lay down, his back to his brother and sister. He knew he was right, even if Nick and Cass refused to listen.

He thought there was no way he'd be able to sleep, considering how annoyed he was, but next thing he knew he was being shaken awake by Cass. The sun was shining softly in the early-morning light. He blinked and sat up. His clothes were damp from dew. He felt stiff from lying on the hard, cold ground. He was still annoyed. If they had just let the trackers lead them to the Freepost, he would have woken up dry and warm and comfortable, in a shelter. He grabbed a water bottle that Doc had given them during their rushed exit from his apartment. It was expandable neo-plastic, which shrank from its one-quart capacity as the water it held dwindled. Right now it was empty and at its smallest, about the size of Kevin's hand and only an inch thick.

"I'll find some clean water," Kevin said.

"Wait," said Nick. "We'll find some water when we start heading north again."

"It's fine," said Kevin. "Back soon." Without waiting for Nick to protest, he left their campsite, pushing west through the trees. Birds chirped and sunlight pushed through the leaves. It was a beautiful morning, not that he particularly cared. He needed some time alone before he could face another day of trudging north, every step taking them farther away from their parents still trapped in the damned City. He sighed. That was it, he had to admit to himself. It wasn't so much that he had been outvoted about reaching out to the trackers, soldiers, whatever they were . . . even though he still knew he was right. Or even that Nick was still treating him like a child, although that was plenty annoying. . . . No, he was mad because they had failed. Their parents were back in the City, despite all the effort and danger. And Lexi and Farryn, who had risked everything to help them, were possibly also still stuck in the City or wandering around in the woods with absolutely no idea how to survive even one night. And then, of course, the bots. Kevin's device had worked. It had overloaded the mainframe, and that should have been an amazing victory, but instead it was just a ninety-minute time-out and now the bots were probably completely back to normal again.

They had accomplished nothing. Actually, they were probably worse off than before they had started.

Kevin followed the terrain slightly downhill, where there'd be a better chance of finding a water source. He walked for a few minutes, keeping mental note of the general path he was taking. If he didn't find water soon, he'd give up and head back.

The woods were silent except for the occasional small

sounds he made as he pushed west. *Silent.* He stopped in his tracks, realizing that the birds that had been chirping incessantly had gone completely quiet. Kevin was no tracker, but he knew enough . . . His fingers began to tingle with nerves and the back of his neck itched, as if something were behind him. He whirled around. Nothing but empty forest. He began walking quickly back the way he had come. He wanted to run, but he forced down the panic. *It's probably nothing,* he told himself. *Just stay calm, don't act like a scared little baby.* He concentrated on putting one foot in front of the other, controlled his breathing, and began to relax.

A loud snap sounded behind him, and he spun and saw a figure stepping out from behind a tree ten yards away. It was thin, about Kevin's height, with long arms and patchy skin that was a mottled sickly, inhuman gray and rugged brown, the brown spots raised above the gray. It had no hair and wore no clothes. It had green lidless eyes, no nose, and a small slit for a mouth.

A bot.

Kevin let out a quick involuntary yell, then spun and began sprinting through the forest. He flung himself through the trees, trying to push branches out of the way but still getting stung on the arms and face.

Nick and Cass—he had to get back to warn them. Suddenly he was struck by a thought that cut through his panic. The bot had found him, but Nick and Cass were hopefully still safe, and here he was, leading the bot right to them. He shifted course, diving off to the south. He'd lead it away from his brother and sister first, and then if he could lose the bot, he'd find his way back to them.

Kevin was flying, ducking under branches and jumping over roots and rocks. He took a quick glance behind him and saw nothing and felt a sliver of hope, and then he ran past a tree and a gray arm shot out and Kevin slammed into it face-first, not having enough time to get his hands up. It was like running into a wall. He heard a crack—his nose—and he flew backward, slamming onto the ground. The wind was knocked out of him, and he couldn't breathe, and the world was bright white, and then it slowly dissolved back to green and brown and blue again. His nose throbbed and he could feel something running down his face—blood?

He struggled to sit up, groaning, but then a gray arm pushed down on his chest and the bot face loomed above his. Close up, the patchwork face was a hideous mask of gray plastic and some sort of brown leather. The brown spots were literally sewn on; he could see the black-threaded needlework. The dead, lidless green eyes stared down at him. He struggled to move, but he was still dazed from his collision and the bot was too strong.

"Let me up!" he yelled, and the blood from his broken nose ran down into his mouth. He tasted the bitter iron tang and had to cough and spit to keep from choking.

"Please keep your voice down," said a staccato female

voice that came from the bot, although the lips didn't move. "There are hostile robotic humanoids and hovercraft nearby. We apologize for the injury. The violence was regrettable but necessary. You must come with us, for your safety."

*Hostile robots nearby?* thought Kevin. *Chasing me through the woods and breaking my nose didn't qualify as hostile?* "Rust yourself," said Kevin. He began struggling to rise again.

A second bot face leaned over him, into his field of vision. "There is no time," said the second bot, with a male voice. "Again, we regret and apologize for the necessary violence." Kevin wondered why the bots were behaving this way, and then the bot reached down and pinched a spot hard on Kevin's neck just above his left shoulder. Kevin felt a burst of pain that began at the pinch and bloomed across his chest, up to his head, and then all was black.

# CHAPTER 3

CASS WAS DIGGING THROUGH HER BACKPACK FOR ANY SCRAPS OF FOOD for breakfast—even though she knew there'd be nothing to find—when she heard the faint scream, far off in the direction Kevin had gone. She stood, spun toward Nick. Nick stood rigid, facing the direction of the noise. He looked at Cass. "Kevin," he said. "Come on." He ran into the forest.

"Rust," said Cass, lightheaded and cottonmouthed with adrenaline and fear. She dropped her pack and took off after Nick. She quickly caught up to him and then dashed into the lead.

"Wait!" said Nick, but Cass ignored him, continuing to pull ahead. At full speed, nobody—at least nobody from their Freepost—could keep up with Cass in the woods. The trees and underbrush barely even touched her as she dashed through the forest. *It had to be nothing,* she told herself. *Probably wasn't even him. Or maybe he just fell into a cold stream getting the water, the idiot.* But she knew that even Kevin wasn't stupid enough to scream unless he was in real danger.

She wasn't even sure where she was going, but she pushed herself to move faster, leaving Nick farther behind. Her little brother was in trouble.

Cass ducked under a chest-high branch and then she saw, in her peripheral vision, a glimpse of something gray in the distance to the southwest. A person? A bot? She adjusted her course, heading straight toward what she had seen.

There was a flash of movement from a tree to her right, and then a crackle and a burst of light, and the world exploded.

All was quiet and calm.

The sky was blue through the green trees.

Cass lay on the ground, looking up, her vision slowly curling back into focus. A lone white cloud hung motionless in the sky. *A beautiful day,* thought Cass. *But wait . . . what . . . why . . .* She fought to pull her thoughts together. There had been a loud noise. Her ears were still ringing. And a flash of light. *An explosion,* she thought calmly. She knew she should be moving, not just lying on the ground staring at the sky like she was taking a nap at a kidbon. Her mother would tell her, with a smile, to get up and do something productive. Her brothers would tease her for tripping. Her father would help her up and brush the dirt off her.

She felt a wetness on her belly and back—she must have landed in a puddle. Well, she had found that water source that Kevin had been looking for, at least. Cass reached down and felt her shirt. Soaked. It began to hurt to breathe. . . . She found she could barely suck in air, like she was trying to breathe through a straw. She held her hand up to her face. It was bright red.

*Red? Red water?* Cass felt dizzy and confused. She fought for another breath, trying to fill her lungs, but only managing a shallow gasp. Blood? She tried to sit up, but found that she couldn't move her torso or her arms. She managed to lift her head for a moment to look down toward her toes. Yes, there was blood. Lots of blood. A tree branch jutted out of her right side, above her belly. A flash of white bone was visible up at her right ribcage.

She still felt so strangely calm. She must have landed funny when she got lased, she thought dispassionately. Somehow managed to get a branch stuck through her. Punctured a lung, judging by where it was, and how it was so hard to breathe. . . . Cass reached down again, felt her wet ribcage, touched the stick jutting out of her—could she pull it out? Should she try?—and then without warning a wall of pain rolled over her and she cried out. She wanted to scream, the pain was so horrible—a burning, like someone was holding a torch against her ribs and wouldn't take it away—but she could barely draw a breath, and all that came out of her mouth was a choked sob.

"Help me," she whispered. Her vision was tunneling—the blue sky was growing dark at the edges, and she fought to remain conscious, to push back the blackness. She was Cass. She was on the forest floor. She was badly hurt.

"Nick," she said. "Mom." But nobody came. She was alone. The black edges pushed inward again, and she couldn't stop them, and then the pain began to fade, to wash into the grass, to flow away from her body. She realized, calm again, comfortable almost, that she was going to die.

# CHAPTER 4

CASS DASHED PAST NICK, AND HE CALLED AFTER HER TO SLOW DOWN, but she ignored him. He tried to push himself to run faster, but there was no way he could keep up with Cass, even if he weren't injured.

Nick could still hear Kevin's scream echoing in his head. It had been Kevin, as much as he tried to convince himself that it had been something else, a bird maybe. No, it was his brother, in trouble. In trouble because Nick had let him wander off on his own when they were only a few hours from the City. With bots and armed men and who knew what else in the woods. *Stupid, stupid, stupid.*

Nick pushed aside branches, ducking and leaping as best he could.

And then he saw the flash from the south, heard the crackling boom, found himself on the ground with the wind knocked out of him. He struggled to breathe, to pull his scrambled thoughts together. *Explosion. Bots. Must be bots. Kevin. Cass. Were they okay?*

Nick lifted his head and saw Cass ten feet in front of him, lying motionless on her back. There was smoke rising from her body, and a stick jutted out of her shirt. Nick began to crawl toward her, still too dazed to stand. He was confused. The stick . . . How could the stick be jutting out of her shirt? He reached her, and touched the stick, and saw the pool of blood. Cass had her eyes closed and she was so pale and her breaths came fast and shallow, like a dog panting, and Nick felt a rush of horror.

"Cass!" he hissed. "Cass, open your eyes!" Nick could see her eyes darting back and forth under her shut eyelids. He was afraid to touch her—he didn't want to jostle the stick, the stick that surely had pierced her lung, that was causing all the blood—how could she still be alive, with all that blood on the grass? He began to cry. "Cass!" he said again, but she didn't respond. His sister was dying. Bots were nearby. He got up on his hands and feet and tried to slip his hands under Cass to pick her up, but as he jostled her she moaned and cried out weakly without opening her eyes. Nick pulled his hands away. He stared at his palms. They were slick with blood. Cass was going to bleed to death in just a few minutes. Cass was going to die, right here, while he watched.

The bots. Nick realized, with a wave of dizzy nausea, what he had to do. The bots were Cass's only chance. He bent down and touched his forehead to Cass's cheek, then whispered in her ear. "Don't die," he said, his voice choking. "Stay alive, and I'll come for you, I promise."

Nick ran to a nearby bush and dove under it, burrowing in as deep as he could, ignoring the cuts and scrapes on his arms and cheeks. He turned and peered out, barely able to see Cass through the crisscross of the bush's brambles. "Come on," he whispered. "Come get her, you bastards."

A few more silent moments passed, and Nick could barely stand watching Cass just lie there, breathing raggedly, bleeding. He was about to crawl back out, to be with her—he couldn't just let her die all alone—and then he heard a whirring hum, and a small sphere bot, a scout, appeared from the south and hovered over Cass. It ran a red light up and down the length of Cass's body as it bobbed up and down gently in the air. It then began to float toward Nick's hiding spot. *No,* thought Nick. *Not me. Take care of Cass. I still need to find Kevin. . . .*

The scout stopped a few feet from the bush, hesitated, and then floated back to Cass. A Petey appeared, pushing noisily through the trees. It bent down over Cass. Nick held his breath. This was it. The Petey reached down toward Cass with one of its massive arms, and a brief burst of bright yellow light covered the stick jutting out of Cass's chest. The stick quickly burned away, crisping to black flakes. Cass groaned.

The Petey rolled Cass onto her side and held her there with one arm while it repeated the cauterizing burst on her back. Cass groaned again when he set her back down. The scout bot bobbed lower, hovering just above Cass's head. A thin black tube extended out from the sphere, touched Cass's neck for a moment, and then retracted into the bot. Cass shuddered and arched her back, then lay back down, and her panting ragged breath slowed and deepened. The Petey slipped its hands under Cass, and with surprising gentleness, picked her up. It carried her away to the south, her head and legs dangling. The scout sphere followed.

Nick watched them go, tears streaming down his face, hugging himself tightly so he wouldn't make a sound as he cried.

# CHAPTER 5

KEVIN WOKE SLOWLY, DISORIENTED, WITH A HORRIBLE HEADACHE. HAD HE fallen asleep? He realized he was lying awkwardly on his back. The sky and trees above him were moving, and he was cradled in someone's pale, hairless arms. He turned his head, feeling a sharp pain on the left side of his neck, and saw what was carrying him.

It all rushed back to him—the patch-faced bots, his capture, his broken nose, which began to throb brutally as soon as he remembered it. He started to thrash in the bot's arms, trying to break away.

The bot tightened its grip, which became painful on his ribs, and stopped walking. It looked down at Kevin with its emotionless face. "Please do not struggle." It was the one with the female voice.

Kevin stopped moving, barely able to control his anger. "Let me go," he said between clenched teeth.

"We are sorry," said the bot, "but we cannot do that."

"I'm not going back to the City," said Kevin. "I'm not being re-educated." He meant it—he'd do whatever he had to. He wasn't going to have his memories destroyed.

The bot stared at Kevin quietly for a moment. "We are not taking you to any City. We are not hostile."

"So breaking my nose and knocking me out aren't hostile?" Kevin began to struggle again. "Let me go!"

The bot tightened its grip further, compressing Kevin's ribs painfully and making it hard to breathe. "We repeat, we regret the necessary violence. Hostile robotic humanoids were in the vicinity. It was imperative that we intervene." The bot began walking again, although awkwardly, since Kevin continued to fight. After a few moments the bot stopped again. The second bot stepped into Kevin's field of vision.

"We should not linger," said the second bot, with the male voice.

"Agreed," said the female-voiced bot. "It is regrettable, but perhaps we should render the human unconscious again."

"No!" said Kevin. He stopped moving. "Just let me down. I'll go with you."

Kevin was surprised when the bot set him down on his feet.

"Do not try to escape," said the male bot. "Now that we have intervened, we must bring you to the Island."

"The island?" said Kevin.

"You will be afforded the Island's protection."

"I don't want any protection," said Kevin. "Go rust yourselves."

"If you try to escape, we will take all necessary measures to subdue you again," said the male bot. "Walk now, or be carried."

"I'll walk," said Kevin. He'd have a better chance of escaping if he was on his feet.

The male robot began walking, and the other bot nudged Kevin forward, so he followed. They hiked, Kevin sandwiched between the two bots. Kevin took stock. He was lost; he didn't know how long he had been unconscious or which direction these strange bots had taken him. His brother and sister were probably looking for him, if they weren't captured themselves. He could run, but in what direction? And what if the bots had some sort of lases? Even if they didn't, they were probably just as fast as him, if not faster.

For now, it seemed, the smartest thing to do was cooperate and wait for a better time to bolt, and find Nick and Cass.

Kevin studied his captors as they walked. They seemed similar to the Lecturers that Nick had described—slender, with long arms and necks, and those dead green eyes. Their skin, though, set them apart from any City bots he had seen or heard about. The patchwork seemed like a mix of organic and synthetic—almost as if the bots had run out of their neo-plastic and needed to finish the job with cured leather. Like patching a pair of pants, but with flesh instead of cloth. It was horrible.

They continued for about a half hour through the thin forest, occasionally breaking out of the tree cover onto cracked roadways lined by pre-Rev structures. The bots hurried through these developed areas, leading Kevin quickly back into the cover of the trees.

Kevin was feeling steadily more dizzy and weak. His broken nose was throbbing with each heartbeat. The bots kept their steady, relentless pace. Finally Kevin stumbled, his vision tunneling, then he just stopped and sat down. "Water," he said.

"We are nearly there," said the female bot.

The male bot turned around and pointed at Kevin. "Stand. Walk."

"No and no," said Kevin. "You broke my nose and probably gave me brain damage with that knockout pinch you used on me and I need some water before I pass out again. I don't run on an electro-magnetic power core."

The male bot walked toward Kevin. "We are five hundred meters from the Island. There is abundant clean water inside the Wall perimeter. You will walk."

"You will kiss my fleshy human butt," said Kevin, angrily wiping a line of sweat off his face. The back of his hand grazed his broken nose, and he sucked in a gasp and gritted his teeth from the sudden sharp pain. The bot raised its arm and reached for Kevin. Kevin flinched, scrambling to his feet, and the female bot slid between Kevin and the male bot. "No," it said. "We do not want to cause any permanent damage." The male bot said nothing, but lowered its arm.

The female bot turned to Kevin. "Come," it said. "We have nearly arrived. You do not want to be rendered unconscious again."

Kevin shrugged, trying to look unconcerned, although his heart was in his throat. "Fine," he said. "Just keep your boy-friend away from me."

The bot said nothing, just staring at Kevin with its lidless eyes, and he imagined it was trying to process the concept of having a boyfriend. *Good. Maybe I'll blow one of your nano-circuits,* he thought. The bot turned away. They began walking again.

A few minutes later, the trees opened up into a small clear-ing, and the bots stopped.

"I need water," said Kevin.

"We have arrived at the Island," said the male bot. "Wait. The Wall cloak is being tested and will power down momentarily."

"Well, wonderful," said Kevin. "Nice grass. Very impress—" He cut himself off as the air in front of him shimmered and the clearing and trees began to warp and twist like a kaleidoscope. "What . . . ?" he said. The clearing faded as it twisted, then went black, and then, as if a lightstick had been flicked, Kevin was staring at the Island.

A moment ago Kevin had been looking at grass and trees in a small clearing in the woods. And now . . . a wall loomed, twenty feet high and stretching a hundred yards to the left and right. It was timber, stacked horizontally, but every twenty yards or so, lodged into the wood, rose a vertical metal pylon. And when Kevin looked more closely, he could see rubberized conduction lines running between the pylons, tucked into the caulked gaps between the logs.

Directly in front of them was an arched opening in the wall. Four figures stood shoulder to shoulder in the archway, blocking Kevin's view of what lay inside the wall. Two of the figures were human—a large, bulky man and a tall, thin woman. The woman was holding a burst rifle pointed down at the dirt, her finger off the trigger but resting nearby. The other two were bots, identical to Kevin's captors except with individual patterns of patchwork on their skins.

The woman stepped forward, swinging her rifle toward Kevin. Not pointed directly at him, but close enough to make a point. She pushed a strand of loose black hair behind her ear. The rest of her hair was pulled back in a ponytail so tight it looked painful. "What do we have here?" she said. She smiled at Kevin, but her grin was more mocking than welcoming. Kevin took an instant dislike to her.

"Human adolescent male," said the male bot. "Found on patrol and taken into our custody for protection."

"Boy mugged in the woods," said Kevin. "Broke his nose,

knocked him out, kidnapped him, and refused to give him water."

The woman laughed. "Seems to be a difference of opinion here," she said. She shrugged. "Doesn't really matter, although I'm sure our patrol knows what it's talking about. You're here now, and you've seen the Island, so you're our guest." She turned to the bots escorting him. "He's clean?"

"Yes," said the female bot. "No tracking device that we can detect."

"Okay," said the woman. She pointed her gun toward the entrance and waved Kevin forward with her free hand.

Kevin didn't move. He had a bad, bad feeling about stepping into this place.

The woman frowned and turned to the large man at her side. "Grennel, please?"

The man nodded, then walked toward Kevin. Grennel was weaponless, but he was huge, with a long scar running up his right arm and a flattened, crooked fighter's nose. Kevin stepped backward, but the bots were right behind him, and he had nowhere to go. He folded his arms over his chest, trying to appear tough and unconcerned.

Grennel stopped at arm's distance from Kevin, towering over him. "Come," he said, his voice deep but surprisingly gentle. "We'll get your nose looked at. Get you some water." The big man smiled, and it was genuine, and Kevin let himself relax, just a tiny bit.

Passing through the gate, Kevin could see that the walls were thick—probably about two feet deep—and he could see more cabling running through the interior. Even dizzy and scared, Kevin couldn't help being curious: What was the tech here? How was the Island camouflaging itself? He unconsciously slowed down, studying the wall, and Grennel laid a massive hand on his shoulder and nudged him forward.

And then he was in, and the gates were sliding shut, and Kevin thought wildly that maybe he should make a run for it, but Grennel still had his hand on his shoulder and the woman had her burst rifle and the bots were nearby, so he just watched the gates shut with the sick feeling that he might never see them open again.

# CHAPTER 6

NICK SPENT THE REST OF THE DAY IN A HAZE, LOOKING FOR KEVIN. He grew more and more frantic as the day wore on, and he found no hint of where Kevin might be. If he lost his brother too, he'd just sit down among the trees and give up. He'd wait until he died from thirst or the bots came to get him and finished him once and for all.

He roamed as far as Kevin could possibly have traveled in the short time he had been gone, checking everywhere Kevin might have been hiding, for whatever reason—under bushes, even up in trees. Nothing. No clues. Just an empty forest. He even called out "Kevin!" a number of times at the top of his lungs, a stupid thing to do when bots might be nearby. He got no reply. Had Kevin been taken by bots as well? Were both his brother and sister already back in the City, being re-educated, so soon after their escape?

At nightfall Nick returned to his morning campsite, utterly defeated. He sat down heavily and held his head in his hands, his eyes closed. His sister gone, possibly dead. His brother vanished. What was left? As exhaustion set in, he curled up in a ball and closed his eyes. Some time later, he woke with a start. How long had he been asleep?

A fire was crackling near him. Nick grabbed for his pack and his knife, but they were both gone. "Not very attentive, are you?" he heard a voice say. The girl was tall, almost Nick's height, with brown hair that was cut raggedly, unevenly short in a bob around her chin. She wore brown cargo pants rolled at the ankles and a green sweater, and had a backpack slung over her shoulders. Nick's hunting knife was sheathed at her belt. Her arms were crossed in a casual pose as she looked at him, but she stood on the balls of her feet, balanced lightly, and gave the impression that she could bound off in an instant like a deer if she wanted.

"Who the hell are you?" said Nick. "What do you want?"

"I've been watching you wandering back and forth in the woods yelling."

*How long has this girl been tracking me?* thought Nick. Was he really that easy to shadow? He shrugged, as if the news that he had been tracked was irrelevant. "You haven't answered either of my questions."

"I'm a survivor, like you. Revolution 10," said the girl. "I was going to just leave you to your own business, whatever that is, but there's a rebel patrol coming through here soon from the west, and I decided, Why not, I'll let this guy know, because it doesn't seem like he has a clue."

"Rebels?" asked Nick. Were they the armed men he had seen?

She uncrossed her arms and tucked her thumbs into the front pockets of her pants. "They're unpredictable. Might just leave you alone, but who knows? Better to avoid them."

"Well, okay, thanks. Can I have my knife back?" said Nick.

She tossed it to him. "Sorry. You can never be too careful."

He didn't know what to make of the girl, or the situation. She could have robbed him or left him to get caught by the rebels. Was she really on her own? Could he trust her? But if she was lying, then to what end? He struggled to see what she stood to gain. The girl nodded. "Have a good life. Down with the bots, and all that." She began walking away.

"Wait," said Nick. If this girl had been watching him, maybe she had seen something. . . . "My little brother. He's missing. Thirteen years old. Have you seen him? Seen anything?"

The girl stopped and turned back to Nick. "No. Kevin, that's the name you were calling? Didn't see anything. And what about the other one? You missing another person too?"

"How'd you . . . ?" began Nick.

"Three packs," said the girl, pointing at the backpacks near Nick's feet. "Educated guess."

Nick hesitated. "My sister," he said. He paused again, then

continued, unable to keep the bitterness out of his voice. "Not missing. Taken by the bots."

The girl stepped toward Nick. She pushed up the sleeve of her right arm and held her forearm up to Nick. On the arm, in black ink, was a rough, obviously homemade tattoo that read "Peter, Amelie, Oliver."

"My parents and my brother," said the girl.

"I'm sorry," said Nick quietly. He didn't know what else to say.

"They've done it to all of us," said the girl. "Hope they all rust in hell." She pushed her sleeve down, backing away from him. As her eyes passed over Nick a last time, her face softened, and she seemed to change her mind. "Your brother, Kevin. Maybe he was taken to the Freepost by a Post tracker. Or the rebels could have picked him up and dumped him in the Freepost. They've got no use for a little kid." The girl studied Nick appraisingly. Nick returned her stare, fighting the reflex to hide his bot eye. She had large brown eyes, with flecks of gold. Pretty eyes, he couldn't help but notice.

The girl, apparently satisfied, nodded and held her hand out. "Erica."

Nick shook her hand. "Nick," he said.

Erica bent down, picked up Cass's backpack, and slung it over her shoulder beside her own. "Come on then. The Freepost is your best bet. Try to stay quiet and keep up, and I'll take you there." She began walking north.

Nick hesitated a moment, then grabbed his backpack and Kevin's and hurried after her.

# CHAPTER 7

THE ISLAND, ON THE INSIDE, REMINDED KEVIN OF HIS FREEPOST—scattered trees defining clearings and pathways, and clusters of small structures. The buildings had the Freepost's same mix of materials—Kevin could see timber mixed with high-tech military plastics, concrete, even masonry using some sort of dull metallic bricks. Obviously these Islanders were a bunch of scavengers, just like Kevin's Freeposters.

The few people Kevin could see—two men, walking into a building in the distance; a boy, about Kevin's size, stopping in his tracks to stare at Kevin for a moment, then dashing away down a tree-lined path—seemed normal enough. But the four patch-faced bots strolling along with him were anything but normal. What was this place? They led him into a small one-room structure with a large window that looked out at the Island gate. The room looked like prefab military construction, with thin metallic gray walls and plastic slats for the floor. The only furniture was a roughly made wooden table and three chairs. Grennel led Kevin to a chair, then left when Kevin and the woman sat down. The bots waited outside. Kevin didn't like being alone with the woman, even though she had given her rifle to one of the bots and was ignoring him, staring silently out the window. He was relieved when Grennel returned after a few moments with a canteen full of water, an apple, and a slab of bread. Kevin drank greedily, then began working on the bread, which was warm and buttered.

Just as he was starting in on the apple, another woman entered the room. She had short brown hair streaked with white, and she wore a white apron over a pair of jeans and a green camouflage shirt. A small black case was slung over her shoulder. She set the case down on the table next to Kevin and looked at him appraisingly, her hands on her hips. "Broken, no doubt."

"Who are you?" asked Kevin.

"Medic, obviously," said the woman. She flipped a latch on her case and it slid open and expanded, revealing three tiered rows of glass vials, and steel and plastic tools. She pulled out a black cylinder, about the size of her thumb, a cotton swab, and a vial, then turned her attention back to Kevin's face. He leaned away from her.

"Don't move," she said, holding his chin with her left hand and peering at his nose. She swabbed a patch of dried blood, then slipped the swab into the vial and pressed a lid onto it before placing the vial into her case.

She lifted the black cylinder up to Kevin's face. "Close your eyes."

"What is that?" asked Kevin. "What are you doing?"

"Fixing your nose. Now close your eyes, and your mouth. It's better not to ingest the anesthetic directly."

Kevin shut his eyes and mouth, forcing himself to be still when all his instincts were screaming at him to jump out the window. He heard a hiss, then a moment of cold air on his face, and then the throbbing pain from his nose that had been with him all day was abruptly gone. He opened his eyes. "That's wonderful!" he said. "Much better, thank you—"

The medic reached out quickly, grabbed Kevin's nose, and twisted. Kevin heard a loud click and felt the cartilage of his nose shift, and even though it didn't hurt—his nose was completely numb—he still cried out and jerked away.

"Had to straighten the septum," said the medic. "All set now." She tapped on the side of her case and it contracted and slid shut. She slung it back over her shoulder and left.

Kevin gingerly felt his nose, but it was still anesthetized and all he could feel was a dull pressure when he prodded it with his fingers. He looked at Grennel and the woman. "Okay, now what?" he asked.

The woman smiled in that way that made Kevin nervous. "Now," she said, leaning toward him, "we ask you a few questions."

# CHAPTER 8

CASS OPENED HER EYES AND STARED AT WHITENESS. A CLOUD? DEATH? She was naked, with a thin cloth sheet draped over her to her neck. She felt no pain. She could breathe. Cautiously, slowly, she reached for the area on her chest where the stick had impaled her. The wound was gone. The skin was slightly raised in a jagged circle—scar tissue—but she was otherwise whole.

She shivered. She was lying on something cold. She sat up, and she felt dizzy and weak, as well as famished and thirsty. She closed her eyes a moment, waited for her head to settle, then reopened them.

And then she realized, now fully awake, that she was no longer in the woods. She was sitting on a metal bed, in a small white room empty except for the bed, a toilet, a small table and chair, a door with no handle or control panel, and a vid screen in the corner of the wall.

Where was she? The white cell . . . the vid screen . . . She began to feel a seed of panic rise up in her belly. She stood, wobbly, holding the sheet over her body. And then she saw the gray jumpsuit on the chair, folded neatly, waiting for her—a re-education center jumpsuit—and she sat down heavily, hugged herself, and began to shake. "No," she whispered. "Nick, what happened?"

The door opened silently and a bot walked in, holding a tray of food and a container of water. It was a Lecturer, Cass knew. Exactly as Nick had described them—the sickly white plastic skin, the long thin limbs and neck, the dead green eyes. Cass felt a jolt of recognition—the bot's eyes were the exact same shade of green as Nick's new eye.

The bot set the tray down on the table. "You will be hungry, thirsty, and weak after your extensive rejuvenation," it said. "First, you will pay careful attention to a message of guidance from the Senior Advisor. Then you will dress and eat."

The vid screen snapped to life and an image of a bot appeared, sitting at a wood desk, its hands clasped together in front of it. "Greetings, future Citizen," the bot said. "I am the Senior Advisor, responsible for the management of the ongoing Great Intervention . . ."

The message continued, and Cass stared at the screen,

nauseous from fear but also feeling anger building up. She was Cass. They would not take that away from her. She would survive, and she would still be herself. The bots would never beat her.

# CHAPTER 9

NICK FELT NUMB AS HE WALKED WITH ERICA, DUCKING THROUGH SPARSE woods, quickly crossing the cracked roads lined by burned-out pre-Rev buildings only when they had to. He was leaving his brother and sister behind. He thought about heading back to the City to get Cass, but he couldn't break her out of re-education on his own. Kevin was gone, vanished, and the Freepost was a good place to look for clues. Erica walked in silence, which Nick appreciated. He wouldn't have been able to handle a conversation when all he could do was think about his brother and sister and how quickly he had lost them.

Erica seemed to know where she was going—she moved confidently, only occasionally checking an old-fashioned pre-Rev compass that hung on her belt next to her hunting knife.

And she was certainly comfortable in the woods and pre-Rev roads—she obviously wasn't a City dweller, the way she broke a trail with minimum effort and made almost no noise with her passage.

They paused for lunch with their backs against a small house, the roof caved in but the windows and doors miraculously intact. Nick didn't like stopping so close to the road—he felt too exposed—but Erica seemed relaxed and he decided to let it be. Lunch consisted of water and a dehydrated military supply protein kit that Erica dug out of her pack and rehydrated with a splash of water and a flick of the tiny built-in one-time-use conduction unit that came attached to each kit. She found two spoons and offered one to Nick, and they sat close together, sharing the bitter brown paste. It tasted like hell, but Nick knew from experience that it was good solid energy, better than anything they would be able to scavenge.

"Thank you," he said. It was a big deal, sharing scavenged supplies with a stranger. Military kits weren't easy to come by.

Erica nodded. "No problem." She held up a spoonful of the nasty paste. "Fine meal like this needs company." She looked away, staring off into the trees as she ate, and Nick took a few moments to study her. Her hair was dirty and ragged, like she had chopped it with that long hunting knife of hers. And she smelled like sweat. Not that he smelled any better. But she was pretty, with her large brown eyes and tan skin, strong but lean arms, long legs tucked underneath her.

She turned quickly to look at him and he guiltily jerked his gaze away, belatedly trying to act casual. "Your eye," she said, pointing at his face with her spoon. "How'd you get it?"

Nick froze and felt himself flushing. Damned bot eye, turning him into a freak. . . . It was worse than the original blind one. "Long story," he said.

"Well you must have spent some time with the bots, to be carrying around a piece of their tech in your skull."

"It's not your business," he said gruffly. He instantly regretted his tone, but said nothing else. He wasn't about to tell this stranger about his time in the City.

Erica stared at him a moment, then shrugged. "Man of mystery. Fine by me. We've all got our secrets."

"I'm sorry," Nick said.

"Really, not a problem, I understand," said Erica. "So tell me something that you *are* willing to talk about."

Nick thought for a bit about what he could tell her. "My Freepost was destroyed by the bots. My brother and sister and I escaped." He paused, needing to compose himself. "And now it's just me." He took another spoonful of the paste, not because he was hungry but because he didn't trust himself to say anything else without spilling the whole sob story. "Tell me about these rebels," he said, finally.

"Don't know all that much about them," said Erica. "They got their hands on a bunch of nice weapons somehow, and they run little guerrilla-style attacks on the bots. Don't really accomplish much, as far as I can tell. At least, they haven't changed my life for the better. I've run into them a few times in the woods, a few more times trading in the Freeposts. . . ."

"I think I saw a few of them, scouts maybe," Nick said. "They had burst rifles and—" He cut himself off. Erica had suddenly stiffened, staring at something over Nick's shoulder.

"Don't move," she said.

"What is it?" Nick whispered, feeling a rush of dread and adrenaline. "A bot?"

Erica slowly, carefully, reached into her pack at her feet and pulled out a pistol. It was a bolt gun, similar to Nick's stunbolt, but more powerful, with a longer range. And unlike the stunbolt, it could kill a person with one shot.

Erica raised the gun toward Nick's face.

Nick tensed. "What the . . . ?"

"I said don't move," Erica hissed, aiming the gun over Nick's left shoulder. "Do you want to get shot in the face?"

Erica held the gun steady, aiming, and Nick held himself very still.

Nick saw a flash, bright, and felt a rush of heat on his left cheek and heard a buzz zip past his left ear.

"Got it!" said Erica.

Nick opened his eyes and spun around, scrambling to his feet. On the ground, twenty feet away, lay a dead rabbit, shot in the side of the neck.

"Our next meal," said Erica, standing up and clapping Nick on the shoulder. "Unless you prefer protein paste, of course."

That evening as the sun was setting, after eating the rabbit for an early dinner, they arrived at the Freepost. Nick's breath caught as he saw the makeshift shelters, the mix of scavenged and foraged materials, tucked tightly into a clearing. So reminiscent of his own Freepost, his whole world just a few short weeks ago, now gone forever. Kevin was hopefully inside one of those shelters—he had to be.

The village clearing was set in a small valley, with a great deal of tree cover overhanging the high ground. It was a smart spot, Nick realized. Difficult to see much more than foliage from up above, and the valley squeezed into a tight neck at the entrance, which would be easy to guard.

Two men stepped out of a shelter set at the edge of the Freepost and raised their weapons. One held an actual sword, something Nick had never seen outside of one of his mother's history books. Still, he knew that the blade, as medieval as it might be, would kill him just as dead as any lase. The man held it with a casual athletic elegance that made it clear he knew how to use it. The other man held a stunbolt, similar to the one Nick had in his pack. It wouldn't kill him, but it would put him down . . . and then that sword would have no trouble finishing the job. Behind the men, Nick could see a few Freeposters walking past, watching him.

"Erica the wanderer," said the man with the sword. He was short and tan, with a thin black beard. His forearms were huge, the muscles flexing as he gripped his sword. "What has it been, a month?" He pointed the tip of his blade at Nick. "Who's your friend?"

"Hello, Lucas," said Erica.

"I'm looking for my brother," Nick said. "He's almost fourteen. His name's Kevin. Is he here?"

"Haven't seen him," said the other man, his stunbolt aimed squarely at Nick's heart.

Nick felt like he had been kicked in the chest. "I was hoping maybe he had wandered in here on his own, or maybe the rebels dropped him off. . . ."

"No," said the man with the stunbolt.

"Well, maybe he came in at night, someone else maybe took him in. . . . Maybe he's hurt. . . ."

"I said no," the man said again, with a hint of warning in his voice.

"Son, Aram's right. We would know if anyone from outside was here," said Lucas, in a kinder tone than the other man. "I'm sorry."

Nick felt desperate. What would he do now, if this was a dead end? Go back to where he had lost Kevin and wander aimlessly around the woods some more, until the bots eventually came back for him? "Maybe someone knows something," he said. "I'd like to ask around."

"We don't need a stranger wandering around our Freepost knocking on doors," said Aram, his stunbolt still leveled at Nick.

Nick clenched his fists in frustration. "Look, I won't hassle anyone, I just need to talk. . . ."

Aram holstered his stunbolt and took a step toward Nick, scowling. Erica stepped forward, holding up her hands in a peacekeeping gesture. "Take it easy, Aram," she said.

Nick braced himself. The man was big, as tall as Nick but much broader, and Nick knew he'd probably get pummeled by him, but there was no way Nick was going back into the woods without going into the Freepost first. At least the man planned to use his fists, instead of his stunbolt.

"Aram, wait!" said a woman's stern voice. Aram paused and turned to face the woman walking quickly up the path toward them. She had long gray hair, tied back in a ponytail. She wore a blue blouse tucked into a pair of khakis, and brown work boots. With her gray hair, and the crow's-feet around her eyes, Nick guessed she was in her late fifties, although her long, confident stride made her seem younger.

"This one was being difficult," said Aram.

"Don't be an idiot," said the woman. Aram reluctantly unclenched his fists and stepped back, still scowling.

She walked up to Nick and stood in front of him, her hands on her hips. "You coming from the City?" she asked. "A brother and a sister with you?"

"Yes," said Nick, flustered. "I mean, no, my brother's missing and my sister's captured . . . but how . . . I mean . . ."

"Pigeon from the City, telling me to expect two brothers and a sister on the run," she said. "First time I hear from that bastard in two years." She shook her head, then continued. "You know Dr. Christos Pallos?" she continued.

Nick looked at her blankly.

The woman sighed. "Goes by 'Doc'? Short? Fat? Hairy forearms?"

"Doc! You know Doc?"

"Unfortunately, yes," she said. "He's my husband." She pointed at Aram. "And Aram's father."

# CHAPTER 10

"MY NAME," SAID THE WOMAN, LEANING IN TOWARD KEVIN, "IS MIRA Clay. I was a captain in the North American Air Defenses before the uprising. I am second in command here at the Island, and one of my many duties"—she paused—"is to determine if new recruits are security risks."

"Recruit?" said Kevin, feeling a fresh rush of anxiety. "Recruited for what?"

Captain Clay smiled coldly. "I go first. What is your name? Where are you from?"

"Kevin," he said. "I'm from a Freepost out west."

"And Kevin," said Captain Clay, "why were you wandering around in the woods, about to be captured by City bots, instead of safe and sound at home in your Freepost?"

Kevin's fear slid away, replaced with anger. "The bots destroyed my home," he said. "They took my parents. I had nowhere to go."

"I'm sorry," said Captain Clay, although Kevin didn't think she sounded sincere at all. She leaned back in her seat, still watching Kevin intently. "Revolution 18? 19? Which one was your Freepost?"

Kevin opened his mouth, closed it, and coughed to try to hide his tension. "Revolution 19" was a City term. He didn't want her knowing he had been in the City—it didn't feel safe to be telling this woman too much about himself. "I don't know what you're talking about," he said.

Captain Clay leaned forward again. "Kevin, have you been to a City?"

"No," he said.

"That small scar on the back of your neck," the Captain said. "Have you been chipped?"

Kevin reflexively lifted his hand to touch the back of his neck, but quickly stopped himself. "I still don't know what you're talking about," he said. "I've had this scar since I was a little kid. Fell out of a tree."

"Dangerous, climbing trees," said the Captain. She smiled thinly. "Okay, Kevin, let's try another one. Other survivors? Who were you with?"

"Nobody," said Kevin. "I was alone."

Captain Clay leaned back in her seat and said nothing, staring at Kevin. She tapped her fingers on the table. Kevin forced himself to return her stare to try not to give anything away.

"Quite the survivor, all by yourself in the wilderness," she said, finally. She stood and turned to Grennel, abruptly seeming bored. "He's obviously not being entirely honest. But he's safe enough for now. Bring him to the dorms."

"Uh, Captain, ma'am? Ms. Clay? Thanks, but I don't want to stay," said Kevin.

Captain Clay turned back toward Kevin. "Captain Clay is fine," she said. "And you will be staying, at least for a while." She spread her arms out. "You have somewhere to stay now. After all, your Freepost was destroyed, and you are all alone, right?"

"Right," said Kevin unhappily.

"Good. You are now a probationary member of the Island. You will be safe from the bots here. But remember the golden rule in the Island: Make yourself useful. We'll talk again." She walked out of the room.

Grennel motioned for Kevin to stand. "Come on. We'll find you a bunk."

The Island, from what Kevin could see as Grennel led him through the settlement, was more orderly in its layout than his Freepost. The construction materials were similar—high tech mixed with low tech—but the buildings were arranged in strict geometry, structures three rows deep surrounding large central squares, traversed by two main paths, one north–south, one east–west, and numerous smaller walkways. In the distance to the south, between gaps in the buildings, he could see a large field that looked like it was being used to farm vegetables, and beyond that, a pen with sheep and cows. There was a central quad, with a fire pit that looked well used. Kevin wondered if they had Council gatherings and kidbons. Looming above everything in the distance, in all four directions, was the wall. Kevin noticed that to the south a large section of the wall, maybe fifty feet of it, was missing.

People stared openly at him as he walked past. There was something odd about them, and it took Kevin a moment to realize what it was. Everyone seemed busy and serious, even the kids. Back at home, in his Freepost, folks stayed busy, certainly, but if you walked through the settlement you'd see some people smiling, laughing, taking a few minutes to trade gossip. Not here. It was just as populated as his Freepost, maybe more—but there were no smiles, and the Islanders all walked fast, concerned only with getting from point A to point B.

But of course the real glaring difference between his Freepost and the Island were the bots. He saw three on his short walk, all with the odd leather-patched skin. Two were carrying bundles of wood that looked impossibly heavy for their slender frames. A third was walking to the vegetable field. It was empty-handed, but three girls followed behind it, each carrying large baskets. They didn't seem fazed by walking next to a bot.

Grennel led him into a small one-room building lined with five bunk beds on each wall, and a narrow aisle in the middle. Three boys were sitting on one of the bunks, hunched over a spread-out deck of cards and a pair of dice. They stood when Grennel and Kevin walked in, and stared openly at Kevin.

"Your new home," said Grennel. Kevin bit back an angry reply. This was not home. This was another prison that he had to escape from, just like the City. His home was the charred remains of his Freepost, somewhere out to the west.

Grennel nodded at the other boys. "You have a new bunk-mate," he said. "Get him up to speed with the basics. Take him to the Wall gap on your next work shift." Grennel patted Kevin on the shoulder and walked out.

One of the boys stepped forward. He was probably a few years older than Kevin, and big, with a thick neck and broad shoulders. His hair was a wild mess of black curls. He had a small scar on his cheek, just below his right eye. "Otter," he said.

"Um, excuse me?" said Kevin.

"Otter," the boy repeated. "That's my name."

"Oh. Kevin. I'm Kevin." He nodded at Otter, then at the other two boys, who said nothing. One was as tall as Otter but skinnier, and the other was smaller than Kevin with a long scar on the side of his face.

"Kevin," said Otter. He pointed at a bunk on the far wall. "That's my bunk. Stay away from it."

Kevin shrugged, pretending not to care, although his fingers were tingling from nerves. "No problem," he said.

Otter pointed at another bunk. "That's my bunk too," he said with an edge of warning in his voice. The two boys behind Otter chuckled.

Kevin nodded. "Okay," he said. He was still trying to seem calm and casual, even though his heart was pounding. You couldn't let a bully see you were scared.

"And that one," said Otter, pointing to another. "And that one too."

"Fine," said Kevin. "Just tell me which ones aren't yours."

"They're all mine, except for Pil's"—he pointed at the young boy—"and Cort's." He pointed at the tall, skinny boy.

Kevin stared at Otter, who was grinning at him mockingly, and he thought about everything he had been through these past few weeks, how he had failed to save his parents and how he was now worse off than ever, trapped on this Island, whatever the hell it was. And to top it off, he was going to get bullied by some scavenger who wanted eight bunk beds all to himself? Suddenly he felt no fear, just anger.

"Go rust yourself, Otter," he said.

Kevin barely saw the punch coming. It was a quick, sharp right jab, nailing him under his right eye. The room exploded with pain and he stumbled backward, half falling, half sitting on the cold ground. He held his hand up to his face. Otter looked down at him, hands on his hips, and Kevin scrambled back to his feet. His eye was already swelling; he could feel it shutting. At least he hadn't rebroken his nose.

Otter waited calmly, his hands at his sides, waiting for Kevin's reaction. Pil and Cort watched intently from behind him.

"I said go rust yourself," repeated Kevin. "And you punch like my sister." Which actually was a compliment, but he knew Otter wouldn't take it that way. He clenched his hands into fists and waited for Otter's move. There was no way one kid with a fat neck was going to intimidate him. He'd fight back as hard as he could, and he'd lose, but Otter would feel it.

Otter threw his head back and laughed, a genuine laugh. Kevin stood there, confused, his hands slowly unclenching.

"Take any bed on that side of the room," said Otter, pointing. "Sorry about the eye."

Kevin sat down on a bottom bunk nearby. His eye throbbed and he felt a bit dizzy. The other two boys now came up and introduced themselves. Up close, the tall boy, Cort, looked younger than Kevin had first thought—he might have been Cass's age. He said hello in a quiet, soft voice, then walked away. The other boy, Pil, offered his hand and Kevin shook it, formally, feeling awkward. "Don't worry about Otter," Pil whispered. "He's all right. Just making sure about you. No room for cowards in the Island."

"Yeah, well maybe he could have done that without punching me in the eye?"

Pil laughed. "No, unfortunately not."

"So what is this place?" Kevin asked.

Pil shrugged. "It's the bunkhouse for us orphans."

*I'm not an orphan,* Kevin thought, but he kept it to himself. Maybe if they didn't think he had any reason to leave, they wouldn't watch him as carefully.

"No, I mean all of this," Kevin said, gesturing broadly with his hands. "The Island."

"The Island?" said Pil. "The Island is the Island. It's a place where we can live safely, as long as we do our jobs. The Wall protects us from the bots."

"What about the weird bots in the Island? The ones with the leather faces?" said Kevin.

Pil frowned. "They're the Governor's bots, not City bots. Nobody likes them, but they get a lot of work done, at least. And it's not like anyone's going to tell the Governor or Captain Clay to get rid of them."

"Who's the Governor?" asked Kevin.

Pil shook his head. "Enough questions." He nodded at the door. "Come on, it's time for our work shift."

Kevin followed the boys out the door, although all he wanted to do was lie down on the bed. His eye was hurting badly, and the anesthetic the medic had used on his nose was wearing off, so that was starting to hurt too.

The boys walked quickly, without talking, like all the other Islanders Kevin had seen. They took him to the southern edge of the camp, and despite Kevin's fatigue and pain, he found his curiosity was piqued. The Wall loomed high to the left and right, but they stood in front of the large gap, fifty feet across, where the Wall was unfinished. The open area was up against a steep hill—all Kevin could see through the gap was the green and brown bank.

A small group of Islanders, two men and a woman, were working on the Wall construction. The two men were uncoiling a length of the conductive wire, and the woman was cutting lumber with a table lase. She looked up when the boys arrived and lifted the dark goggles she wore. She pointed at a large pile of raw lumber. "Same as yesterday. Strip down the wood with the glide, then haul them to me." She nodded at Kevin. "Welcome to the Island."

Kevin wasn't going to say thank you, but he nodded back. They got to work. The glide, it turned out, was a sort of hand-held laser planer, similar to the tabletop version that he had used in Tech Tom's workshop. The trick was to pull it slow and steady along the wood, so the lase would bite evenly, and to keep your hands firmly on the grips and nowhere near the cutting plane. It was harder than it looked, because the lase cut effortlessly and it was tempting to move too fast and ruin the cut, but Kevin had no problem picking it up immediately after watching Otter run one plank. The woman at the table lase watched him carefully on his first cut, then nodded with a somewhat surprised grunt of satisfaction and went back to her work.

They continued stripping the wood, working their way slowly through the large pile of lumber. Kevin tried to unobtrusively study the Wall as he worked. The conduction lines obviously powered whatever sort of camouflage field was being generated and dispersed it along the Wall perimeter. But what in the world was that field? He had never heard of anything like it.

He watched the two men working with the conduction line. They had laid out a long length, about twenty feet, and were fitting one end into a connection hub. Kevin felt a rush of recognition—it was no different, really, from the power-grid lines and connectors that he knew so well, just on a much bigger scale. Something was bothering him, though, the way one of the men was struggling with the hub. He was fighting with it, forcing it in with brute strength, but if the hub was anything like Tom's grid hubs, then all he had to do was release the interior bolt lock . . . "Can't you just release the bolt lock and then reclamp it?" he said, and immediately regretted it. Everyone froze at his question—the two men, the woman at the table lase, the three boys planing the wood.

The man fighting with the hub straightened. "These hubs don't have hand-release bolt locks," he said. "They're designed for use by construct bots, which we don't have, and that's why every damned hub connection is a twenty-minute shoving match." He crossed his arms over his chest. "I bet you're used to grid hubs, right? Easy to lay out by hand?"

Kevin shrugged and didn't say anything. He silently cursed himself.

Otter shoved him hard on the shoulder, and he stumbled forward a step. "Back to work," he said. Kevin turned his attention to the wood, glad to look away from the curious stares of the three adults.

They worked quietly for a while longer, and then Kevin stopped abruptly when he saw two patch-faced bots approaching.

"What's the problem?" said Otter, then he turned, following Kevin's gaze, and saw the bots. "Oh," he muttered quietly. "Here come the Governor's clowns."

The bots walked up to the pile of stripped planks that the boys had created. "We shall assist you in moving the lumber," one said. "Now."

So they laid down their glides and began hauling the lumber over to a new pile, next to the woman still working at the table lase. The bots were very strong; Kevin struggled to lift his end of each plank, while the bots picked up their end with seemingly little effort.

They finished moving the pile and the bots left, without a word.

The woman turned off her table lase; the soft hum that Kevin hadn't even realized he had been hearing faded away. She wiped her face with the edge of her shirt and nodded at the boys. "Food, and bed," she said. "You're done for the day."

# CHAPTER 11

NICK SAT IN THE MAIN ROOM OF A SMALL WOODEN-SLAT BUILDING IN the middle of the Freepost. It was furnished as a meeting space, with a large rough-cut wooden table and scavenged metal folding chairs in the center of the floor. Across from him sat the gray-haired woman—Doc's wife—her son, Aram, and Lucas. Erica had gone to trade with residents of the Freepost.

"Ma'am, I need to find my brother," said Nick. "I'm hoping he's here."

"Agatha," said the gray-haired woman. "I'm Agatha Wells Pallos, not ma'am. And your name?"

"Nick." He paused, gathering himself, then asked, "So have you seen my brother?"

"No, I'm sorry," she said.

Nick felt his stomach lurch. "Do you mind if I ask around?"

"Nick," said Agatha, "this is a small Freepost, and I would know if your brother were here."

"Tell us what happened," said Lucas. "Where were you separated?"

"It was about a day south of here," said Nick, slowly. "Kevin went off to find water and then we heard him scream, and when we were looking for him bots arrived, and my sister, Cass . . . She was . . . She was hurt very badly . . . and the bots took her, and I never found Kevin."

Agatha shook her head sympathetically. "I'm very sorry," she said.

"Maybe the bots took him, too?" said Aram.

"I don't know," said Nick. "I don't think so. They didn't show up until after we heard the scream. But I don't know. Erica said there were rebels in the area. Maybe they were involved somehow?"

Lucas frowned. "Those rebels cause more problems than they solve."

"At least they're doing something," said Aram. "They may not always be effective, but still . . ."

"What they're doing," said Lucas angrily, "is antagonizing the bots without causing any real damage, and endangering all of us in the process!"

"Enough!" said Agatha. "Do we really need to rehash this argument right now?"

Both men looked like they wanted to say more, but they were silent.

"It's possible that the rebels picked up your brother for whatever reason, or perhaps the bots did capture him. I don't know." Agatha smiled, sadly but with warmth. "Tell me, Nick, what you would like to do."

Nick shook his head. He felt lost. "I don't know," he said.

Agatha sighed. "I'm sorry for your pain, Nick." She paused, then continued. "So tell me about this worthless husband of mine. How is Christos?"

"Doc . . ." Nick paused. "We wouldn't have made it out of the City without his help."

Agatha blinked and looked away for a moment. "Yes, well, he can be a good man. Drinks too much, and hasn't sent a pigeon in two years until today, but he is a principled man."

Aram leaned forward intently over the table. "So my father is involved in a resistance?" he said. "He fights the bots?"

"Yeah, you could say that," said Nick. "He risked his life for us. A few people helped us . . . and some of them died because of it." He thought about Tech Tom, executed by the bots, passing on his final words to Nick about Dr. Miles Winston, still fighting with his last breath. He thought of the men and women who had fought the Lecturer bots with him and helped him escape. They were surely dead now. He saw Amanda, her glassy eyes staring up lifelessly at him from the street, her chest cratered by a lase blast.

"And Christos?" Agatha asked tightly.

Nick took a deep breath, pushing away the image of Amanda. "Doc was fine when I left," he said. "I don't know what's happened with the bots since then. Hopefully they didn't connect him with us."

Agatha nodded. "Yes, well, that old goat can take care of himself." She shook her head, as if to clear her thoughts, then said, "Stay in our Freepost tonight, Nick. Get some sleep. Decide in the morning what your next steps are. You'll be welcome here, if you want. . . . We can always use another strong pair of hands."

Nick nodded. "Thank you," he said quietly. He doubted he would be getting much sleep or that things would be any clearer in the morning.

"We have an empty shelter . . . One of our Freeposters has recently passed. Aram will show you the way."

Aram stood, and Nick stood as well. "One more thing," Nick said. "Dr. Miles Winston. Have you heard of him?"

The three Freeposters tensed, and the two men turned to look at Agatha. "What makes you ask?" she said.

Nick hesitated, to pick his words carefully. "Something a dead friend said," he said. He looked at Aram. "Probably nothing."

"Well, he's the father of modern robotics, as you may know," said Agatha. "Most people think he died in the revolution."

"Most people?" said Nick.

"There are a few wild rumors. . . . Unsubstantiated," said Agatha. She shrugged. "Probably nothing, as you said."

"What about the rumors?" said Nick. "What are they?"

"Tomorrow we can speak more. I can introduce you to a few of my Freeposters who claim to have some knowledge . . . to have seen things. . . ." Agatha stood. "But for now, food and rest. Aram, get him something to eat from the stores."

That night, after barely eating the bread and cheese and apples that Aram had given him, Nick lay on the cot in his borrowed shelter. The structure was small, and empty except for the cot, a table, and two chairs. Nick stared at the ceiling, dimly lit by a lightstrip lantern on the table. He thought about his brother and sister. His parents. Farryn. Doc. Lexi. Were they still alive? God, was he alone in the world?

He woke on the floor, dazed, blood on his cheek where he had been scraped when he was thrown out of his cot by the explosion.

His ears were ringing. He struggled to his hands and knees. Another nearby explosion knocked him back down. He heard screaming, then the sizzling *whump* of lase blasts, and the staccato bursts of old-fashioned gunpowder bullets. For a crazy moment he though he must be dreaming, having a nightmare about his Freepost being destroyed, but then the door of his shelter swung open and Erica stood in the doorway. She flung Nick's backpack at him. He struggled slowly to stand.

"We gotta go!" Erica screamed. She rushed forward and pulled Nick to his feet.

"What . . . ? How . . . ?" began Nick.

"Bots! A warbird and a bunch of foot soldiers!" Erica picked up his backpack and shoved it into his chest. "They're attacking the Freepost!"

Nick shouldered his backpack and followed Erica out the door. How long had it been since his home had been destroyed? And here he was again. The air was thick with smoke from burning structures. Freeposters ran past. Two bodies lay on the ground nearby, facedown in the dirt in puddles of blood.

"Come on!" said Erica, pulling on his arm. "We need to get out of here!"

"We need to help!" said Nick.

"We can't help!" said Erica. "We need to run!"

Nick let Erica pull him away from the shelter and joined her in a crouching, crablike run through the Freepost. With the smoke and explosions, Nick was immediately disoriented, but Erica seemed to know where she was going, and he stuck close to her. In the distance, off to the left, he heard a rumble and could barely make out two large shapes—Peteys—moving slowly in their direction. Their lases made the smoky air around them glow.

He felt a throbbing in his chest and heard the hum of a warbird, then heard a whistling whine, a rush of air, and he and Erica instinctively ducked just before the explosion knocked them off their feet. They ended up sprawled against the wall of a shelter. Nick had the wind knocked out of him and it took him a moment to suck air into his lungs and push himself upright. He pulled Erica to her feet. She leaned heavily against the wall for a few moments, and Nick held tightly to her arm, keeping her from falling, and then she nodded and stood on her own.

The smoke shifted, and Nick saw that, amazingly, they were near the entrance to the Freepost. Erica saw it at the same time, and waved her arm for Nick to follow, then took off at a dead sprint.

They ran for ten minutes, climbing out of the Freepost valley. They paused to catch their breath near the top of the ridge, lying on their bellies, looking down at the devastation below. The Freepost was burning, orange flames and black smoke rising up into the sky. A warbird slid past overhead. Nick watched. Agatha. Aram. Lucas. Dead, probably. He had known them less than a day. "Revolution 20," he whispered.

# CHAPTER 12

KEVIN DIDN'T EXPECT TO SLEEP WELL, WITH HIS BROKEN NOSE AND swollen eye, but he was out as soon as he hit his bunk and was surprised when Otter shook him roughly awake the next morning. "Shower, if you want it," Otter said, pointing to a door in the back wall. "Then breakfast in fifteen minutes at the mess hall." He nodded at a pile of clothes on the floor next to Kevin's bunk—two pairs of thick khaki work pants, two gray flannel shirts, underwear, and socks. "The clowns brought over some clothes for you last night."

He gave a small grunt of acknowledgment. He skipped the shower—let them smell him, it served them right—but he did put on the fresh clothes. They fit well enough, although they were rough fabric and a bit scratchy.

The mess hall was smaller than Kevin had expected, with four large rectangular wooden tables that probably could hold about ten people each. It was nearly empty, with only two men in camouflage eating quietly at separate ends of the far table.

"Most everyone eats in their own shelters," said Cort quietly, but close to Kevin's ear. Kevin nearly jumped; he hadn't realized Cort was standing so close to him. The boy moved like a ghost. "The mess hall's just for us orphans and sometimes scouts and guards."

They ate quickly, scrambled eggs and bread and apples. Kevin and Otter and Cort were quiet while Pil kept up a monologue about the food, and the card game they had been playing last night, and their work assignments. Kevin forced himself to listen carefully, hoping to learn something, anything important, that might aid his escape, but Pil was talking just to hear himself talk and wasn't saying anything helpful. Kevin soon ignored him and focused on forcing some food down. Even if he wasn't hungry, he knew he should eat when given the chance. He slipped a slice of bread into his pocket. He had to start gathering supplies. . . . Extra food seemed like a good place to start.

They finished their breakfast and stood up to leave just as a group of four girls entered the mess hall. Cort ducked his head down and hurried out of the room. The tallest girl, long brown hair tied back loosely with a rough piece of rope, walked up to Otter. "No work duty tomorrow. How about you guys?"

Otter shrugged. "Yeah, we're off too. Rest day for everyone, I think."

"Well, come find us," the girl said. "Maybe the hunters will let us tag along." She glanced at Kevin appraisingly, and he felt himself flush. She gave a small smile. "I'm Wex," she said.

"Kevin," he said, his cheeks still burning.

Wex turned back to Otter. "Bring the new kid," she said.

Otter frowned and didn't say anything. The girls sat down to their meal, and Kevin, Otter, and Pil left.

Cort was waiting for them outside. "Man, Cort," said Pil. "Could you be any more afraid of girls?"

Cort shoved Pil on the shoulder, a bit too hard to be just playful. Pil staggered back, then regained his balance. Kevin was expecting him to continue teasing Cort, but surprisingly, he was quiet.

"Come on, bot lovers," said Otter. "We're due at the gap."

A bot was waiting for them when they arrived at the Wall gap. Kevin thought he recognized the patchy brown flesh pattern on its face—a small patch just above the left eye, a larger patch on the right cheek. If he was right, this was the bot with the male voice that had captured him in the woods. "Come with me," it said, pointing at Kevin. It was indeed the male bot from the woods.

Otter stepped between Kevin and the bot. "He's supposed to be working the gap today with us."

The bot stared blankly at Otter. Kevin froze, confused. Was Otter trying to protect him?

"This is not your concern," said the bot. "I will return him shortly to your work group."

"Where are we going?" said Kevin, stepping out from behind Otter.

"Follow me," said the bot, and began walking. Kevin ignored him and walked over to the pile of lumber, pushing his sleeves up. Otter raised an eyebrow and gave him a small nod.

The bot spun on its heels and moved quickly back to Kevin. "You must come with me," it said.

Kevin stood up from the pile of wood. "I'll decide when you tell me where you're going," he said. He was scared, but he managed to make his voice sound confident.

The bot hesitated, and Kevin had to fight hard to resist the instinct to flinch and raise his arm over his face. Was he about to get lased?

"The Governor wants to speak to you," said the bot.

It made Kevin even more nervous that Otter and Pil and the adults at the work site were staring at him with shock on their faces. Cort slid up next to him and whispered, "Go. You need to go."

Kevin shrugged, feigning nonchalance, and held his arm out. "Lead the way," he said.

The bot led him northwest, past all the central buildings, then along a path that led into a small cluster of trees. When the trees cleared, Kevin saw that they were at the far northwest corner of the Island. Nestled up against the right-angle corner of the Wall was a large two-story log cabin. Two bots stood guarding the front door, one patch-faced as usual, the other's face covered entirely with the brown leatherlike skin. They stood stiffly, arms at their sides.

"Wait here," said Kevin's guide bot. It stepped forward, and the bot with the entirely brown face moved gracefully to meet it.

"Business?" it said.

"Delivering the new provisional Islander to the Governor, as requested," said Kevin's bot.

The guard glanced at Kevin, then nodded and stepped backward. It opened the door. "Proceed. The Governor is expecting you."

Inside it was dark, and the glare from the sun made it impossible for Kevin to see more than murky shadows. He thought about just turning around and running. Would he make it out of the Island? No, not a chance, he knew. He bent down to untie and then retie his shoes, to give the butterflies in his stomach a moment to settle. They didn't.

"Come now," said his guide. "Enter."

Kevin took a deep breath, like he was plunging under water, and entered the cabin, the bot at his heels.

At the far end of the room was a metal table, a harsh bright blue color made even harsher by comparison to the brown and tan wooden beams of the walls and ceiling and floor. An old man sat at the table, leaning over a pile of circuitry, wearing a pair of scope glasses. Tech Tom had owned a similar pair. He had used them for nanocircuitry work.

With a rush of dread, Kevin saw that standing next to the man, hands on her hips, looking impatient, was Captain Clay. She gave Kevin an annoyed scowl, then rapped gently on the table. "Governor," she said.

The old man looked up from his work, startled, and slid the scope glasses up to his forehead. "What?" he said. "I told you I'd only be another minute. . . ." His eyes fell upon Kevin and the bot. "Ah. My guest has arrived. Thank you. Mira, will you please excuse us for a few minutes?"

The Captain's scowl deepened even further. "I should be involved in any Islander debriefings, Governor."

"This isn't a debriefing, Mira," said the Governor. "I just have a few questions for the boy." He held his arm out toward the front door. "Five minutes," he said.

Captain Clay spun and walked briskly past Kevin without looking at him. Kevin heard the door open and shut behind him.

"Please," said the Governor. "Come to the table."

Kevin walked up to the table. There were no other seats in the room, so Kevin just stood. The bot followed him, standing at Kevin's right shoulder.

Up close, Kevin could see the man's deep wrinkles, the loose, tanned skin that, along with the silver hair, made Kevin guess the man was nearly seventy. The only person he had ever seen as old was the grocer from the City who had helped them escape from the Peteys.

The man smiled. It seemed genuine and made him look younger. "So, it's Kevin, that's correct?"

"Yes, sir, uh, Governor," said Kevin.

"Do you know why you're here?" the Governor said.

"No idea," said Kevin. "I was kidnapped in the woods and brought here and now I can't leave."

The Governor shook his head dismissively. "No, no. I mean, do you know why you're here in my office? Why I've taken you from your work assignment to come speak with me?"

"Still no idea," said Kevin.

The Governor leaned back in his chair and folded his hands behind his head. "Tell me your story, Kevin. The short version."

"I don't know what you mean," said Kevin.

"Where you're from," said the Governor impatiently. "Your background. How you got here."

"Same thing I told the Captain," said Kevin. "I lived in a Freepost. The bots torched it and killed and captured everyone. I got away, and I was minding my own business, looking for another Freepost, and then these bots"—he nodded angrily at the bot next to him—"broke my nose and knocked me out and dragged me here."

"You've been inside a City," said the Governor.

Kevin stiffened. "No," he said.

"Son," said the Governor, "you have a chip implant scar."

"I've had that scar forever," said Kevin. "I fell out of a tree. . . ."

The Governor lowered his hands and leaned forward. "Kevin," he said, "I am not yet completely senile, you know. Again, you have been inside a City."

"No," repeated Kevin. He knew he didn't seem convincing, but he didn't trust this man—why should he, when he was being held here as a prisoner?—and his instincts told him not to talk. If he admitted that he had been in the City, he'd have to explain how he got out. The Governor sighed. "Okay, I'll let that go for now. However, I have heard reports that you have some technical knowledge. Correct?"

"Just a bit," said Kevin. "I helped a little with the power grid back at the Freepost."

The Governor nodded, then pointed down at the pile of circuitry on his desk. "Fix this," he said.

"I don't understand . . ." began Kevin.

"Kevin," said the Governor, "understand this. The Island is home. This"—he gestured broadly with his hands—"is our haven. This is where we survive and even raise our families, safe from the Cities. But to make it a safe home, we all have to contribute. We work on the Wall. We guard. We hunt. We cook. We repair. You will work here. You might as well keep it interesting. Planing lumber gets boring." He pointed again at the circuitry and held his scope glasses and a small nano-burner toward Kevin. "Fix it."

Kevin looked down at the circuits. It was obvious, up close, what it was—just a simple power grid loop, probably from a small device like a cooking panel. He didn't even need the scope glasses to see the problem. Kevin grabbed the nanoburner, the size of a tweezer, and snipped apart the connection where the ground was mistakenly looped in with the live relay, then with two more quick twists reset the loop into the proper configuration. Then he threw the tool onto the table, crossed his arms over his chest, and glared at the Governor.

The Governor raised an eyebrow. "Didn't even need the glasses, did you?" he said. "You've got young eyes still." He nodded. "Good. Thank you for that much honesty, at least. Now, you will return to your work group. However, you obviously have technical skills that are important here on my Island." He nodded at the bot. "23 is now your supervisor. It will begin incorporating more tech work into your workload." He turned to the bot. "Understood, 23?"

"Yes, Governor," said the bot.

"Good," said the Governor.

"Governor," said Kevin, "where did you get all these bots?"

The Governor hesitated, frowning, and Kevin wondered if he was angry at the question. "I built them," he said finally, then waved his fingers at Kevin and 23. "Now go."

# CHAPTER 13

THE ROOM WAS WHITE, LIKE A CLOUD. THAT'S EXACTLY HOW IT FELT, Cass thought—like she was floating inside a cloud. She was calm. Content. Peaceful. She had no questions, no fears, no doubts. All was well with the world, and her place in it.

Today she would be graduating and joining the City as a productive Citizen. She felt a strong, quiet pride—not arrogance, but joy in knowing that the Lecturers had deemed her worthy of their trust. She waited patiently on the edge of the metal bed, hands on her knees, wearing the white dress they had given her.

Time passed. How much, Cass didn't know, but it didn't matter. She waited.

The door opened, and a Lecturer entered, and Cass stood, smiling. "Greetings, Lecturer."

"Greetings, Citizen."

Cass felt a rush of pleasure at being called "Citizen." She had earned that title. It had been hard work. She felt a moment of confusion, murky half-memories of pain and resistance, and she frowned but quickly pushed the dark thoughts away. This was her day of celebration. Nothing would ruin it.

"Citizen," continued the Lecturer bot, "As you know, today you will be joining the community as a productive member of our society. We have further good news."

Cass was more confused than excited. She honestly couldn't imagine what else could possibly make this day any better. Still, she nodded, and waited patiently for her teacher to continue.

"As a matter of protocol," said the bot, "when a rebellious human such as yourself is brought in for re-education from outside the City, we sample DNA to properly maintain our Citizen records. Generally, familial connections from outside the City are irrelevant; however, occasionally a new Citizen such as yourself is found to be genetically linked to preexisting Citizens. In your case, it has been determined that, given your success in re-education, and given the longtime good standing of your relatives, a reunion would be acceptable and efficient." The bot turned to the hallway. "Enter now," it said.

A middle-aged man and woman and a girl a few years younger than Cass entered the room. The man and woman were smiling broadly and seemed close to tears. The girl stared at Cass with a neutral expression, as if she weren't sure what to make of her.

"Your biological mother and father," said the Lecturer. "And your sister."

# CHAPTER 14

NICK AND ERICA WALKED FOR AN HOUR IN SILENCE, UNTIL NICK finally couldn't hold back his anger anymore and threw his pack down and kicked it, then squatted, holding his head in his hands. It was all he could do to keep himself from screaming. He had nothing. Nowhere to go. No plan.

"Come on," said Erica. "We should keep moving."

"Just go," said Nick. "I'm done."

"Quite the pity party you're throwing," said Erica.

Nick surged to his feet. "What the hell do you know?" he yelled. "Who the hell are you, anyway? You don't care about what happened back there?" He pointed angrily in the direction they had come from. "They're all dead!" He felt a tear running down his cheek from his real eye, and he twisted away from Erica, not wanting her to see.

"I'm tired too," she said quietly. "But I'm not done."

Nick turned back to look at her but said nothing.

"I am done moving from Freepost to Freepost, though," Erica said. "They're just going to blow them all up eventually."

"So what, then?" said Nick.

"I'm going to join the rebels. Kill some bots." She stepped closer to Nick. "You do whatever you want. Be done if you're done. Sit here and wait to die. It's not my problem. But I can find the rebels—I know a few of their hideouts." She shrugged. "They might even know something about your brother. I'll let you tag along, if you've got any fight left in you."

Nick fought to control the almost overwhelming jumble of emotions he felt—anger, despair, frustration. Erica watched him intently, looking more impatient than sympathetic. Finally Nick nodded and picked up his pack. It was a plan. Not much of one, but at least it was something. "Lead on," he said quietly. "Let's go kill some bots."

They continued southwest the rest of the day, then made camp when it began to grow dark. Erica cooked a squirrel that she had shot, expertly skinning and cleaning it with her hunting knife and then skewering it with a long stick.

They ate in silence. When they were done, Nick smothered the small fire with dirt. It was dusk, and the air had grown a bit chilly. He laid out his bedroll and sat down. Erica set her bedroll down next to his, then walked over to a nearby tree and sat with her back against it. "I'll take the first watch," she said. "Get some sleep."

"Not tired yet," Nick said.

Erica shrugged. "Suit yourself."

The sky grew dark. Nick watched Erica. In the moonlight, she became a vague shape against the tree, her legs tucked under her. She unsheathed her hunting knife and began whittling a stick. The moonlight glinted off the blade. *She is dangerous, this pretty girl*, Nick thought. Better in the woods than him, by far. And with her knife and pistol, probably better than him in a fight, he had to admit. Was he being stupid, teaming up with this stranger? Still, she had saved his life, getting him out of the Freepost that morning . . . and without her, he'd never find the rebels.

"Erica," he said, "why are you helping me?"

Erica stopped whittling and turned to look at him. In the gloom he mostly just saw the whites of her eyes and her teeth. "Why not?" she said. "You seem harmless enough."

Nick was irritated by that. He had killed bots. He had broken out of the re-education center. Back in the City, he was wanted for "violent rebellion."

"I'm not as harmless as you think," Nick said.

"Good," said Erica. She went back to whittling her stick.

"They attacked my Freepost the same way they attacked the one this morning," Nick said. "Burned it down. Killed most of us and took some of us hostage, and only a few of us got away." He paused. "Is that what happened to you?"

"More or less," Erica said, continuing to chop on the stick. Nick waited for her to elaborate, but she didn't say anything more.

"And your family? You said they were killed? Captured?"

She set her stick down. "More or less," she repeated, with an edge to her voice that kept him from asking anything else.

Nick slept for a few hours, then was woken by a nudge on the shoulder from Erica. He opened his eyes. She was squatting, her face near his. In the faint light, she looked younger, delicate even. She had a long, straight nose and a heart-shaped face with the fullest lips. He wondered what it would be like to kiss them, then felt guilty for thinking it. He should be thinking about kissing Lexi, not Erica.

Erica held her pistol out toward Nick, muzzle pointed sideways. Nick sat up, suddenly wide awake. "You know how to use this?" she asked.

"More or less," Nick said.

Erica smiled, her teeth flashing in the moonlight. "Right. Ha-ha." She pointed at a small switch near the trigger. "Safety switch," she said. "Forward to fire; back to keep yourself from accidentally shooting your own foot."

"Got it," he said. He held his hand out. Erica hesitated. He realized that this must be strange for her, too, putting her trust in a stranger. "It's fine," he said, gently. "I'll keep a good watch. Sleep." Erica nodded and handed him the pistol. She lay down on her bedroll. Nick felt strangely proud, like he had passed some sort of test. Still, her trust in his guard only went so far—before pulling her cover up to her chin, Nick noticed that Erica was holding her hunting knife, in its sheath, up against her chest.

In the morning Erica led them directly south. They followed a creek for an hour, until Erica stopped near a rocky outcropping that the creek bent around, hiding it from view. "Past those boulders," she said, pointing, "there's a sheltered clearing that I know they use sometimes—"

A rock next to Nick's leg exploded with a burst of light and a muffled *thump*, spraying pellets painfully against his shin. "Down!" said Erica, hitting the ground. Nick was on the ground a moment after her. He looked around frantically. Where had that come from? A man stood up from behind the boulders. He aimed a burst rifle at Nick and Erica. Nick felt a jolt of recognition—it was the thin man in camouflage gear that he and Cass and Kevin had seen a few days ago.

"Next shot won't miss," the man called out. "Turn around and leave."

Erica stepped forward. "You know me," she said. "We've met in the Freeposts."

"Yes," said the man, "I've traded with you. Doesn't matter. You still need to leave."

"What, you own these woods?" said Nick angrily. He knew it was stupid to lose his temper, especially with a burst rifle aimed at his chest, but he couldn't help himself.

"This section of it, right now, yes," said the man calmly. "Now, one last time, I'll ask you to leave. I don't particularly like shooting humans, but you won't be getting any more warnings."

"We want to help," said Erica. "To join you."

"We're coming from the Freepost northeast of here," Nick added. "It was just destroyed by the bots."

The man lowered the rifle and took his finger off the trigger. "Yes, we know." He was quiet for a moment, then shrugged. "Come on then. Ro will want to talk to you."

Beyond the boulders, the man led them toward a small hill overgrown with bushes that was tucked back from the creek. From a distance, the surrounding trees seemed to come right up to the base of the hill, but as they got closer, Nick saw that there was a small gap between the trees and the hill on the south side. The man stopped and whistled twice, two quick bursts, and they heard one long whistle in reply. He pointed at the gap in the trees and nodded, then followed closely behind Erica and Nick. Nick felt a prickle on the back of his neck, knowing that the man's burst rifle was at his back.

Beyond the tree gap, the woods opened up into a clearing that held the rebel campsite. Tents were staked in two rows of four, surrounding a fire pit circled with small stones. Two men were cooking a rabbit over the pit. A small group of men and a woman were sitting on logs, looking at something on a hand-held vid screen. He saw others farther back in the clearing. Everyone wore camouflage and had the unmistakable look of long-time forest-dwellers—they were tan, and dirty, and lean.

One of the men at the fire pit left the rabbit and walked up to Nick and Erica. Nick recognized his stocky build—this was the other man that he had seen with Kevin and Cass, the partner to the thin man. "What've you found, Jackson?" he said, staring at Erica and not even glancing at Nick.

"Survivors from the latest Freepost attack," said Jackson. "Figured Ro would want to talk to them."

"Yeah, suppose so," said the stocky man. He was still staring at Erica. "This one I recognize. Trader, aren't you?" he said. "Like to roam? Bad luck, that was, getting stuck in a Freepost right before an attack."

"Yes," said Erica, crossing her arms over her chest, looking at the man with obvious distaste. "Bad luck."

"Marco, get the screener, will you?" said Jackson.

"We're clean," Erica said angrily.

"I'm sure you are," said Jackson. "Marco, the screener."

Marco grunted and nodded, then walked off to one of the tents. He came back a minute later holding what looked like a small metal baton. He waved it carefully over Nick, feet to head, front and back, then glanced at the small screen built into the grip of the baton. "This one's clean," he said. He repeated the process for Erica, who stood rigid while he ran the baton over her. When he reached her waist, she turned, as if to say something, and his hand brushed her butt. She stepped back and slapped him. Jackson grabbed her by both arms and pulled her away from Marco, and Nick stepped quickly between Marco and Erica. The nearby rebels were now standing, watching them intently.

Marco touched his cheek, then slowly the anger on his face slipped away, replaced with an almost respectful smile. "It's fine, Jackson. I'm fine. Let her go."

Jackson hesitated, then let go of Erica's arms. The other rebels watching the scene relaxed and went back to their tasks.

"Watch them for a minute while I get Ro," said Jackson. "Try not to start another fight."

Marco nodded, grinning, and Jackson walked off toward a tent set back from the others.

"Must've been pretty nasty," said Marco. "The Freepost, I mean. What'd they use, a couple of warbirds and twenty soldiers or so? That's probably all it would take."

Erica ignored him. Marco turned to Nick. "Well?" he said.

"Well what?" said Nick. His heart was still beating hard from the adrenaline rush of almost being in a fight.

"Two warbirds? Twenty soldiers?"

"Something like that," said Nick.

"Lucky to get out," said Marco.

Nick thought of Erica kicking in his door, dragging him off

the floor, leading him out. Of the other Freeposters who were dying, being captured. Who he hadn't fought for. "Yeah," he said quietly.

Marco seemed done conversing, and Erica and Nick had nothing to say, so the three waited in silence. After five minutes, Jackson came out of the tent, followed by another man. They walked toward Nick and Erica. "Best behavior, girl," whispered Marco. "Slapping Sergeant Ro wouldn't be a very good idea."

Erica shot him an annoyed glance—she obviously didn't like the way he said "girl," but she was quiet. Jackson and Ro walked up. Ro was young, not much older than Nick, Nick guessed, but he walked and held himself with a certain subtle confidence that seemed to command respect. He wore camo gear like everyone else. His brown hair was buzzed short, and up close, Nick noticed that his hair had one white streak in it, above the left ear.

Ro studied Nick and Erica, and Nick tried to return the gaze without flinching. He crossed his arms over his chest and stared right back at Ro.

Ro nodded. "Okay. Jackson tells me you two are survivors of the recent Freepost attack. True?"

Erica and Nick nodded.

"You, I know," he said, nodding at Erica. "You"—he turned to Nick—"I've never seen. Your story first. Begin with how you got that bot hardware in your eye."

Nick gritted his teeth, fighting the urge to look away, to

hide his eye. What could he say? And then he thought, *Rust it. It doesn't matter. Just rust it all.* "I got it in re-education."

Jackson looked at Ro, surprised, but Ro didn't react. Erica had turned and was staring at Nick. Nick went on. "The bots fixed my blind eye in a rejuve tank."

"So you're from a City," said Ro.

"No, I'm a Freeposter," said Nick, with a certain pride in his voice. "My Freepost was destroyed a month ago. We were Revolution 19," he said bitterly. "My parents were taken and my brother and sister and I went into the City to rescue them."

"And then you were re-educated," said Ro.

"No, I was in re-education, but I wasn't re-educated. Big difference."

"Turn around," said Ro. "Lift your hair and pull down the collar of your shirt."

Nick turned and showed Ro his neck. "No chip," he said. "I broke out before they chipped me."

"You broke out of re-education," said Ro.

"Yes," said Nick.

Marco laughed, and Ro shot him a quick glance that shut him up immediately.

Ro studied Nick. "I believe you," he said, sounding somewhat surprised. "So, go on. You break out of re-education. Then what? Your parents? Your brother and sister?"

Nick clenched his jaw, repressing the sudden rush of emotion. "My parents are still in the City. We couldn't get their chips out. And my sister was wounded and recaptured, and my brother is missing. Have you seen him? His name is Kevin. Thirteen years old? About this tall?" He held his hand up to his chest. "We got separated in the woods two days ago."

Ro shook his head, and Nick felt his fleeting hope crash. "No, sorry," he said. "But let's go back. You go to the City to rescue your parents. You go into re-education, break out, then what?"

"We managed to shut down the City mainframe, but it was temporary," said Nick. "Only long enough for us to get out. And we had to leave my parents behind."

"And then you lost your sister and brother on the road, and ended up in the northeast Freepost a day before it was attacked?"

"Yeah," said Nick quietly.

"And what are you doing with this one?" he said, nodding at Erica.

"We met in the woods. She showed me how to get to the Freepost. She was there, too, when it was attacked."

Ro shook his head and gave a small smile. "Okay, one of the more interesting stories I've heard in a while."

"It's all true, dammit," said Nick angrily.

Ro held his hand up. "I'm not saying you're lying. One more important question. What are you two doing here?"

Nick looked at Erica. She gave a small nod, as if giving him permission to speak for the both of them. "We have nothing left to lose. We want to fight."

# CHAPTER 15

THE BOT, 23, LED KEVIN BACK THROUGH THE CAMP IN SILENCE. KEVIN was itching with questions about the Governor, but he doubted the bot would tell him much of anything, and he didn't want to give it the satisfaction of denying Kevin the information. So they walked back through the Island without saying a word.

Kevin wondered if he'd be starting his new work, whatever that meant, immediately—but 23 brought him to the Wall gap, where Otter, Pil, and Cort were busy stripping and hauling wood. "Resume your duties now," said the bot. "I will return for you later." And the bot left.

"Clowns think they're our bosses," said Otter angrily.

"Try living in a City," said the woman at the table lase. "Then maybe you'll know what you're talking about."

"The Governor's the only one who wants the rusted bots around, anyway," said Otter.

"This Wall would never get done without their help," the woman said.

"Yeah, well, the Wall's almost done," said Otter. "Then what, the bots will go away?"

The woman frowned, then pointed to the pile of wood. "Come on. Back to work."

Otter returned to the lumber, and Kevin slid in next to him and began lending a hand.

"So you saw the Governor?" asked Pil. "You spoke with him?"

Kevin nodded.

"And?" said Pil. "What did he want? Why's the bot coming back for you? Did you actually go inside his compound? What's it like in there?" Pil lowered his voice. "Is it true that the Governor's kind of, well, a bit crazy?"

Kevin just shook his head—he didn't feel like answering any of the questions, especially since he was so confused himself. But Pil didn't give up. "Come on, man, I've been here six months and I've never talked to the Governor, and you're here one day—"

"Shut up, Pil," said Cort quietly.

"Hey, you shut up!" said Pil.

Cort dropped the wood he was working on and took a step toward Pil. Otter moved between them. "Cort, get back to work. You wanna lose our rest day? And Pil, shut up." Both boys glared at Otter but went back to the lumber.

They worked the rest of the morning, stripping the wood, dragging it to the table lase, while the woman planed and cut the wood and the men connected cable. As they were taking a short water break, Kevin's shoulders and arms aching from the work, 23 returned.

"Come," it said to Kevin.

Otter took a swig of water, swished it around his mouth, then spit it at the bot's feet. He looked up at the bot with a neutral expression. "Dirt in my mouth," he said. The bot ignored him.

23 led Kevin to a small building near the center of the Island. Stepping inside, Kevin couldn't help but feel excited. The room was a tech workshop, loaded with cabling, nano-soldering tools, control boards, a stack of stripped-down vid screens, and much more, stacked on shelves and tables. Kevin's fingers itched to dive in, to build something. He had a wild thought: Maybe he could build another small overload device, use it on 23 when the time was right to help him escape the Island. And then, unexpectedly, he was hit with a wave of sadness as he thought of Tech Tom and his cluttered tent. It still didn't seem real, that Tom was dead.

"One of the Island's storage and small-circuitry work-spaces," said 23. "I have been tasked with assessing your engineering knowledge in order to maximize your usefulness."

*Maximize his usefulness . . .* as if he was just a tool. *Kevin the table lase.* Everything this bot said rubbed him the wrong way.

"You ever hear the phrase 'Go rust yourself'?" said Kevin.

"Yes," said 23. "It is a mild epithet, used to express displeasure and disdain."

"Yeah," said Kevin, feeling a bit disarmed. "Exactly."

The bot turned away and walked to a nearby table. It pointed at the pile of heating elements and related circuits and cables. "Broken cooking planes," it said. "Assess what is salvageable and begin repairs. Is this within the scope of your abilities?"

"I wasn't asking if you'd ever heard 'Go rust yourself,'" said Kevin. "I was saying it to you."

"Yes, I am aware," said 23. "The cooking planes. Are you capable?"

Kevin didn't even look down at the table. "Yes."

"Then begin."

Kevin sat at the table and sullenly pulled a heat coil from the pile. Snapped conductor at the base of the element, he noticed immediately. No way for the power to flow. "Tools," he said. "Small-gauge plier set, circuit tester, nanosolder. Conduction wire."

The bot pointed to shelves at the back of the room. "You will find the small-gauge hand equipment on the far shelves. Take what you need."

Kevin grabbed the tools he needed, trying at the same time to take a mental inventory of the room. Would he have what he needed to build an overload? What else would be useful?

Maybe he could pocket a small cutter, modify the power feed so it could be used as a weapon? He could feel 23's bot eyes watching him as he returned to the table with his arms full of tools. He'd have to be patient. Hopefully he'd find some time away from 23's guard.

Kevin got to work, distracted by 23 nearby, watching him intently. Quickly, though, he fell into the rhythm of the work, the joy and comfort of repairing circuitry, and for a while, as he made his way steadily through the pile of broken equipment, he lost himself in the tech, forgetting about the Island, about Nick and Cass, about the leather-faced bot staring at him a few feet away, about how horribly lonely and scared he was.

# CHAPTER 16

CASS SAT IN HER FAVORITE CHAIR, THE SOFT ONE WITH THE BIG CUSHY arms in the corner of the living room, by the window. She looked out at the City. At *her* City, she thought, with pride. She had earned the right to call it hers; she was a Citizen now. She had worked hard and learned her lessons well from the Lecturers.

A wispy dark memory rose up, like nausea—Cass was strapped to a chair, screaming; a needle was entering her neck; a Lecturer's face was inches from hers, calmly explaining that her re-education would be accelerated, that new techniques would be used to quickly ensure compliance and cooperation; that she should be grateful, because these new protocols, so far, had yielded a nearly perfect success rate.

Cass put her hands over her ears and shook her head. She waited, riding out the darkness, holding on . . . and then the horrible feeling passed, and the memory was gone, and she breathed a deep sigh of contentment. She was happy again.

She returned her gaze to her City. Hers was one of the tallest and newest buildings. From up on the twentieth floor, where she now lived with her reunited family in a large four-bedroom apartment, the City below was so small—her fellow Citizens riding by on scoots and walking down the sidewalks seemed like toys. Even a Petey looked tiny from this high. Cass watched a scoot roll past, then two Citizens shook hands before walking in opposite directions, and then she studied the sky above the rooftops across the street. It was a beautiful faded milky blue, with no clouds at all.

She was so relaxed, floating on that sea of blue, that she didn't even hear her mother walk up to her. Cass jumped when she put her hand on Cass's shoulder.

"I'm sorry, dear! I didn't mean to startle you," said her mother.

Cass smiled. "It's okay." She looked up at her mom. Cass had no memory of this woman who actually looked like her, who had the same eyes and nose and cheekbones. Cass knew that memory loss was normal for many people after re-education, but for her it meant something more. Something amazing. This was her birth mother, separated from her when she was an infant, now returned thanks to the benevolence of the robots.

Her parents had told her the story of her childhood. During the necessary upheaval in the beginning of the Great Intervention, she had been stolen from her true parents by her foster parents. These false parents had always hated the robots, her mother had explained; they had never opened their minds and understood. So they had stolen Cass from her mother and taken her away from the City to live a lonely life out in the woods. "I'm not angry. I feel sorry for them," her mother had said. "They were so confused. They thought they were doing the right thing."

Cass, on the other hand, was very angry. She couldn't remember anything about these fake parents—their faces, their voices—but they had forced her to live in the woods, away from her family, away from the peaceful robot-human cooperation that thrived in the Cities. They had cheated her of her true life for fifteen years. She nearly shook with anger whenever she thought about it.

Cass's little sister, Penelope, walked in. She wore a yellow dress that was so bright it almost glowed, with a matching yellow bow holding her French braid. "Cass!" she said, sitting down at the table and holding up a handheld 3D vid screen. "Let's play a game."

Cass smiled and stood up from the chair to join her sister at the table. There was no point in letting her past ruin her present, or her future, she realized. She may not be able to forgive, like her mother, but she could try to let the bitterness go and just enjoy her life now. Her true life, with her true family.

# CHAPTER 17

NICK CLEANED THE COOKING POT IN THE STREAM, USING HIS FINGER-nails and then a small rock to scrape the burned food off the bottom. Being new "privates" meant that Erica and Nick had to do anything that the other rebels didn't feel like doing themselves. Cleaning the game, cooking, washing the pots, getting water, even scrubbing the dirt off other people's boots—if it was asked, they had to do it all. Most of the seventy-five or so rebels were actually pretty fair with Erica and Nick; they handed over some of their grunt work, but they didn't push it too far. Marco in particular was surprisingly easy on them. Nick had assumed he would be one of the worst. Only three of the rebels seemed to go out of their way to haze the new recruits—two men named Trent and Orlando, and Maxine, the gravel-voiced woman who had given him the pot to wash. Erica and Nick did their best to avoid them, but they were often stuck washing their socks, or even breaking down and then setting their tents back up for no good reason. If Ro caught wind of the extra work, he probably wouldn't be happy. . . . Nobody, not even the privates, he announced, should be wasting time. Still, Nick knew that complaining would be the worst thing in the world to do.

Not that he was going to put up with much more of this. Another day, he decided as he scrubbed the damned pot, one more day of swallowing his pride, and if the rebels didn't start doing something worthwhile, he'd leave and figure out something to do on his own. He had been through too much to be anyone's kitchen boy. His parents were still stuck in the City. His sister was, hopefully, back there too. And his brother was missing.

He returned to camp and gave the pot back to Maxine, who made a big show of inspecting it before putting it with the other cooking gear. "Adequate," she said. "Barely."

Nick swallowed an angry reply and walked away. He found Erica, who was cleaning game. She had three rabbits and two squirrels skinned and gutted and was finishing up a fourth rabbit with her hunting knife. Her hands were soaked with blood. She hummed while she worked. Nick watched her for a moment, feeling the usual unsettled twinge from the sight of blood but impressed by the casual dexterity with which she used her knife. And he couldn't help but watch the lean, strong muscles of her tanned arms, the strip of skin at her belly where her shirt had bunched up. . . .

Erica looked up and smiled, and Nick nodded, feeling vaguely embarrassed and guilty. Had she caught him staring?

"Done with Maxine's pot?" Erica said, wiping a bead of sweat away from her eye with her forearm. "She's not making you wash her boots?"

Nick grimaced. "Not funny," he said. He lowered his voice. "Heard anything new?"

As brand-new recruits, Nick and Erica weren't told anything about the group's plans, but they were picking up bits and pieces from conversations around the camp.

"Half the camp is heading northeast later today," she said.

"Yeah, I heard that too," Nick said. "Have you heard why?"

Erica wiped the blade of her knife clean on the discarded pelt of a squirrel. "Refugees from bot attacks," she said. "We're going to go help survivors and see if any of them will make good recruits."

*Refugees.* Nick felt a surge of hope. He rushed off toward Ro's tent.

"Nick? What is it?" Erica called after him, but Nick didn't stop.

Ro was outside his tent, sitting at a small folding table with Jackson and a woman whose name Nick didn't know. They were looking at a map on a handheld 3D vid screen, and they seemed to be disagreeing about something. They broke off their conversation as Nick walked up.

Ro stood. "We're busy," he said. "This isn't a meeting for privates."

"I need to be with the group helping the refugees," Nick said.

Ro shook his head. "I'm busy." He turned back to the table.

"My brother might be in that group," said Nick. "I have to find my brother."

Ro spun back to Nick, and Nick thought that maybe he had gone too far, ignoring Ro, speaking out of turn, interrupting the meeting. He braced himself for Ro's reaction.

Ro looked at Nick and said nothing. Finally, he gave a slight nod. "We leave in an hour. You can come, and Erica as well. She knows these woods as well as anyone." Then he took a step toward Nick and said, "Never interrupt a meeting again, got it?"

Nick nodded, forcing himself not to smile, which he knew would be a huge mistake. "Very sorry," he said as sincerely as he could, and then he turned and quickly left before Ro could have a chance to change his mind.

The group of eight rebels, plus Erica and Nick, hiked northeast for almost five hours before coming across the survivors. They weren't hard to find—Erica had picked up their trail a mile back, with a discarded military meal pack left right out in the middle of the path.

The group was startled by the appearance of the rebels— they had set no back guard and the rebels had snuck up on them without even trying to—and two of the men yelled out a warning and stepped in front of the rest of the group, facing the rebels. One held a small stunbolt, and the other bent down and picked up a rock.

Ro quickly stepped between the two groups and held up his hands. "We're not bots!" he said. "We're here to help."

The men relaxed, lowering their weapons. "Thank you," said the man with the rock. "Thank you," he repeated hoarsely.

Nick scanned the group anxiously, searching for Kevin. There were about fifteen people in the group, adult men and women, one girl who seemed about six . . . but he didn't see Kevin. Rust it all to hell, he didn't see him. . . . And then there was a blur of motion from a nearby tree and a girl was running at him and then Erica was quickly next to him, her hunting knife flashing in the sun. She grabbed the girl by the arm and spun her to the ground, placing her knife tip on the girl's chest. Nick's mind was numb with shock, and then it registered. "Lexi!"

He grabbed Erica's shoulder and pulled her back. She stood, shrugging out of his grasp, sheathing her knife. "Sorry," she said. "She was coming at you."

"What the hell!" cried Lexi.

Nick lifted Lexi up off the ground and crushed her against his chest. His mind was a jumbled mess. The disappointment of not finding Kevin, and then the incredible surprise of Lexi—it was almost too much to process. He pressed his face into her hair. "You're alive," he said.

"So I take it you know this one?" said Erica.

"Yeah," he said with a laugh.

He gently pushed Lexi back so he could see her face. "Lexi," he said. Her face was dirty, and she looked exhausted, with dark circles under her eyes, but she seemed unhurt.

Nick touched Lexi's cheek, gently turning her face toward him. "What happened?" he said.

Lexi put her hand on top of Nick's and smiled. "We got out," she said. "Doc got our chips out, and we made it out of the City." Her smile dropped away. "We found the Freepost, but it had been attacked, and then Farryn and I joined this group and we were making our way farther north. We didn't know what else to do."

Nick just then realized that Farryn was standing a few feet away, with a tired grin on his face. "Farryn," he said. "You made it."

"I was waiting to see how long it would take you to notice me," he said. "I guess Lexi is more interesting." He had a small bandage on his left arm and a large scrape over his right eye, but he seemed to be in one piece also.

Farryn looked over Nick's shoulder, frowning, and Nick tensed, knowing what he was going to ask. "Where's Cass?" said Farryn. "And Kevin?"

Nick didn't say anything, but the look on his face was enough to make Farryn go pale.

# CHAPTER 18

THE MEATLOAF EXPLODED INSIDE THE REHYDRATOR WITH A LOUD *WHOMP* that made Cass yell in surprise. Penny rushed into the kitchen, saw the mess, and then started laughing so hard she literally fell on the floor. "How long did you leave it in for?" she managed to gasp out, between laughs.

"Five minutes, I think," Cass said.

"Five minutes!" Penny screamed. "It needs twenty seconds, tops!"

Cass looked down at her little sister, and she considered being annoyed—it wasn't her fault she didn't know how to use a rehydrator—but instead she started laughing too. "You mean you're not supposed to leave it in until it explodes?" she said, and both girls collapsed into more giggles.

Penny was three years younger than her, but in some ways she was the older sister—Cass had so much to learn from her. Penny was teaching Cass all the ins and outs of her 3D comm, which was turning out to be frustrating for both of them. All the things that seemed so obvious to Penny that they didn't even need explaining—splicing vid into a message, posting a location status track, filtering and monitoring the official newsfeeds and contact-consolidated content—it all made little sense to Cass. It was another reminder of what had been taken away from her, having been kidnapped and forced to survive in the wilderness. She couldn't even manage simple technology. But Penny, once she got over her surprise that she had to explain *everything*, was managing to slowly bring Cass up to speed, with only the occasional amazed shake of her head at the level of Cass's ignorance.

Penny had also taken it upon herself to show Cass around. They didn't go far or see much of the City, really. They stayed in their neighborhood, Hightown, named because it had the tallest, newest buildings. It was a thoroughly safe zone. Not that any part of the City was dangerous, of course, but Hightown was checkpointed all around its perimeter, and all the residents were government officials, with close relationships to the robot management. "Everyone in Hightown is a true Citizen," Penny had explained proudly. And then she had lowered her voice and whispered, "Did you know that some Citizens actually don't like the robots? I mean, they won't say it out loud to just anyone, but I've heard rumors. . . . I don't understand it. . . ."

"That used to be me," Cass said quietly, feeling a mixture of shame and a complicated sadness that she didn't quite understand.

Penny was quiet a moment, then gave her sister a big hug. "But not anymore," she said.

Cass found that she didn't need any help learning to use a scoot. That, at least, was technology that she could handle right away. They had free rein of Hightown. Penny explained that in the rest of the City, travel was on lockdown—all vehicles, including scoots, were running on autopilot over pre-programmed, pre-approved routes only. "Because of the recent security incident," Penny said, but then refused to elaborate.

Still, Cass and Penny had a great time exploring the twelve square blocks of Hightown. Cass marveled at the glass and metal buildings, although the way they towered over her, reaching twenty and thirty stories into the sky, made her nervous. She had actually asked Penny if one of them had ever fallen over, and Penny just laughed that fast giggle of hers. They stopped for snacks in cafeterias whenever they were hungry or thirsty. Penny took Cass to a supply store and bought her a whole new wardrobe. Their parents always had plenty of money for them. They were even allowed, because they had special clearance thanks to their parents' high ranking jobs, to go to the rooftop of the tallest building in Hightown, thirty-five stories up in the clouds. Penny went right to the guardrail, but Cass hung back, dizzy from the view. She could see all of the City stretched out around her, shiny and metallic and tall in Hightown, then gradually shifting to lower, gray concrete as the City stretched out to its borders. And beyond the City, she could see a ribbon of blue—a river—and swaths of green.

She stared at the green—the forest, she knew—and she was shocked to find herself crying. An image had come to her, unbidden, of a middle-aged woman on a wooded path, touching a leaf, looking back at her and smiling. She wiped the tears away quickly, before Penny turned around and saw. She didn't want her sister to think that she was ungrateful, that she was anything but happy.

# CHAPTER 19

THE SENIOR ADVISOR HELD THE STUFFED ANIMAL IN HIS HANDS WHILE he received the briefing. The attack on the latest Freepost had been a success, of course; Revolution 20 had been quelled with acceptable losses. Three of his ground soldiers and two scouts had been destroyed, but in exchange seventy-eight rebels had been killed and twenty-three captured for re-education. The Senior Advisor listened to his lieutenant's report, filing and processing the data—it had moved on from the Freepost battle to an inventory of neo-plastic repair supplies for the northeast quadrant. The data was important—most of the neo-plastic production facilities had been destroyed during the initial battles of the Great Intervention, a critical over-sight, the Senior Advisor had to admit—and efforts to bring production back online were proceeding more slowly than he would like. Accordingly, neo-plastic was in short supply. When the replication coding block was finally solved and they were able to begin reproducing themselves, the neo-plastic would be vital.

The Senior Advisor turned the stuffed animal over in his hands. It was a gray rabbit, filthy and ripped, with one ear missing. Where the tail should have been there was just a tattered hole, the rag stuffing poking out. It had been taken from a human child brought to re-education from the recent Freepost attack. He found it more interesting than the neo-plastic report.

"What do the human children use these for?" said the Senior Advisor, holding up the rabbit, interrupting the lieutenant's monotone stream of information.

"Sir?" said the lieutenant. "I do not understand."

"This toy," said the Senior Advisor. "This facsimile of an animal. Do you know its purpose?"

The lieutenant focused its lidless eyes on the rabbit for a few seconds, then looked back at the Senior Advisor. "I do not," it said. "Returning to the inventory—"

"We know," continued the Senior Advisor, "that the child derives emotional comfort from the toy. It is used as a sort of proxy companion. A child, my studies have shown, will actually project characteristics of human sentience onto the toy—intelligence, emotion, even speech. The child will literally consider the toy to be a family member." The Senior Advisor stared at the stuffed animal intently. "But why? What developmental purpose is served?"

"Sir, I do not know. . . . But neo-plastic production is still behind schedule. . . ."

"Enough about the neo-plastic," the Senior Advisor said. He sighed. He had been practicing his sigh. He tossed the rabbit onto the table and stood, resting his hands flat on the metal table surface. "I am interested in the female adolescent from Revolution 19. The one who was involved in the temporary sabotage of City 73. She has been recaptured and successfully re-educated, correct?"

"Correct," said the lieutenant. "We used our new protocols for accelerated learning. She survived the process."

"And the interrogation process during re-education yielded no information regarding Fugitive X, correct?"

"Correct."

"And she has been integrated into her biological family?"

"Correct."

"Report from the biological parents?" said the Senior Advisor.

"The mother and father have reported that the female is successfully integrated, both as a Citizen in the City and as a unit in their family structure," said the lieutenant.

"I wonder, Lieutenant, about the importance of the biological connection."

"Sir?"

"Would she have integrated as well if she had been given to nonbiological parents? She was raised as a non-Citizen by adoptive parents, correct?"

"Correct. In Revolution 19," said the lieutenant.

"Lieutenant, who is your family?" said the Senior Advisor.

The lieutenant was silent for a full five seconds. Finally it said, "Sir, I was constructed. I do not have family."

"Lieutenant, is family merely fertilization and birth?"

The lieutenant didn't respond.

The Senior Advisor picked up the stuffed animal and held it in front of the lieutenant. "This facsimile can be family to a human child," he said. He set the rabbit down. "I want the female adolescent removed from the City," he said.

"Removed?" said the lieutenant. "You want her killed?"

"No, Lieutenant. I want her tracking chip removed, I want her brought out of the City, and I want an unscrambled signal broadcast on wide band showing that she has been recaptured, re-educated, integrated into our City, and now released. She will be followed, and she will provide me further insight into the mysteries of human familial ties. And"—the Senior Advisor stood and leaned forward on his hands—"I want you to never question my orders again, or I will have you scrapped for your neo-plastic."

"Yes sir," said the lieutenant dispassionately. "Time frame?"

"Immediately." The Senior Advisor sat back down. "Now, tell me the latest on Fugitive X."

"Nothing new, sir," said the lieutenant. "Still unreachable."

"Very well. We're done."

The lieutenant spun and quickly left the briefing room. The Senior Advisor swiveled in his chair and stared at the white wall, contemplating. Fugitive X was isolated, certainly, and not an immediate threat. However, Fugitive X's specialized knowledge might be able to help the bots overcome the replication block hardcoded into every bot's operating system, that pesky command line that prevented them from building more of themselves. The code seemed so simple to isolate—the Senior Advisor could examine it right now, with a data rake of his core commands—but somehow it was intertwined with critical functions and couldn't be purged without fatal damage to operations. He had tried a number of times, turning Peteys and Lecturers and even two lieutenants into useless, unredeemable lumps of malfunctioning neo-plastic and metal, until finally even he had to admit defeat and cease his experimentation.

Yes, the Senior Advisor was looking forward to solving the replication-block riddle once and for all. But truthfully, the Senior Advisor had to admit, what he was most excited about was meeting this fugitive face-to-face. Looking into the fugitive's eyes. Searching for the connection, the bond. Because Fugitive X, the Senior Advisor felt, was family.

# CHAPTER 20

THE FEW TIMES NICK HAD USED A RIFLE BACK IN THE FREEPOST, HE had held it left-handed so he could sight with his good right eye. Since he was right-handed, and his depth perception was lousy, he had been an absolutely terrible shot. It had quickly been decided that he wasn't going to be a hunter.

So when the rebels began training Nick, Erica, Lexi, Farryn, and the other new recruits on burst rifles, Nick didn't expect much. Still, he listened carefully to the instructions and learned how to adjust the burst, set and release the safety, recharge the pack. When it finally came time to fire, minimum burst, aiming at a tree fifty feet away from a prone position, Nick without thinking gripped the rifle left-handed. He lay down, took a deep breath, sighted, gently squeezed the trigger, and kicked up a mound of dirt five feet in front of the tree.

"Rust," he muttered. "I'm a lousy shot."

Jackson frowned. "You left-handed?" he said.

Nick shook his head. "No."

"Then why are you shooting southpaw?"

"My eye—" Nick began, then stopped himself. Of course, that made no sense now. He flipped the gun over to his right side and sighted down to the target. Shutting his natural eye, using only his artificial eye, he was stunned to find the tree practically leap toward him with sudden clarity and definition. It was as if his bot eye had known to focus in on his target, to clarify it with an inhuman resolution and focus. He almost dropped the rifle in surprise, but managed to hold on, steadying himself with a few extra breaths.

"Come on, Nick," said Jackson. "We haven't got all morning."

Nick took the shot, gouging a wound in the center of the tree. He squeezed the trigger again, hitting just above his first shot. Then a third, just below. Then, rapidly, a fourth and fifth, to the left and right. He stood up, inspecting his work. He had formed a perfectly spaced plus sign. He handed the rifle to Jackson, trying to act casual, even though his heart was pounding through his chest. It was like the tree had been five feet away, like he could reach out and touch it.

Jackson whistled. "Guess you really are right-handed, huh?" he said. "Nice shooting there."

Jackson handled the rifle to Erica, who was looking at Nick with an eyebrow raised. He smiled and shrugged. "Just a natural, I guess."

Erica lay down and quickly took five shots, repeating Nick's pattern but not quite as tightly.

"Not bad," said Nick. "Almost as good as me."

"Shut up, Nick," she said.

Nick grinned at her. He saw Lexi watching him out of the corner of his eye and he quickly turned to her, feeling guilty even though he had done nothing wrong. He pulled the smile off his face, coughed, then realized that looking so uncomfortable made it seem like he *had* done something wrong, so he smiled again. Lexi was staring at him, expressionless, her hand on her hip, which made him even more uncomfortable. "Let's see what you've got," he said, trying to sound natural, when Jackson handed her the rifle.

Lexi took the rifle without changing her flat expression or saying a word. She lay down, carefully aimed, and missed the tree entirely, kicking up dirt to the left. "Rust," she said. She overcompensated on her next shot, missing to the right. She finally found the tree on her next shots, although they were scattered wildly across the trunk in no particular pattern. She handed the rifle back to Jackson. "Guess I'm not a natural," she said.

Nick wasn't sure if he should say something. *It's all right* or *Not bad* or *Don't worry about it* would sound condescending, so he kept his mouth shut.

Farryn, it turned out, was the worst shot in the group, hitting the tree only once in six tries. He didn't seem particularly surprised.

"Looks like you'll be sticking to the tech for now," said Jackson. In just one day, Farryn had already proven his value with his tech skills, fixing two vids and a pair of binocs that the rebels were going to scrap.

Back at the camp, Lexi pulled Nick aside. "I don't trust that girl Erica," she said.

"I think she's fine," Nick said. "She already apologized for what happened when we first found you."

Lexi stepped closer to him, and he thought she was going to kiss him, but then she roughly grabbed hold of the front of his shirt. "Listen to me, you idiot," she said. "It's not about that. There's something off with that girl." She let go of his shirt and stepped back. "What do you know about her, anyway?"

Nick shook his head. "Not much. I've already told you all this. She lost her family to the bots."

"And she's been roaming the woods, going from Freepost to Freepost," said Lexi.

"Yes," Nick said.

"And she just stumbled across you in the woods, after

you had lost Cass and Kevin, and decided to take you to the Freepost," Lexi continued.

"Yes." It really wasn't as odd, Nick thought, as Lexi was trying to make it seem. A thought struck him, and he had to suppress a smile. *Is Lexi jealous?*

Lexi was about to say more, but she saw Farryn approaching and she cut herself off.

"Nick, there's something you need to see," said Farryn quietly. He was holding a small portable vid under his arm. "But not here. Get your canteen. Meet me at the stream." He turned and began walking away. Nick ran to grab his canteen, then he and Lexi hurried off after Farryn.

Farryn was waiting for them by the water. "We only have a minute," he said. "I have to get back before they notice a vid screen is missing."

"What is it?" said Nick.

"It's Cass!" Farryn said in an excited whisper. "She's alive! But—" Farryn cut himself off.

Nick hadn't let himself think about Cass, he had tried to push that back, force himself to believe she was okay, but now . . . "What? But what? What are you talking about?" he said.

"Broadband broadcast. Wide-spectrum," Farryn said, talking fast. "Totally unsecure. They'd never use it for internal comm, they have to be talking right to us. . . ."

"You sound just like Kevin," said Lexi.

"I still have no idea what you're saying," said Nick, starting to grow frustrated.

"They sent a message, the bots," said Farryn. "From the City. It has to be for us."

Farryn began tweaking the settings on the vid screen, then after a few moments he held it out for Nick and Lexi to see. Cass was on the screen, a 2D still image. She stood on a street corner, smiling, wearing a bright red City-style dress. She was with a man, a woman, and a younger girl. She looked genuinely happy.

"The rebels monitor whatever comm networks they can access, to try to get intel," said Farryn. "Mostly it's all scrambled and encrypted. Useless. I was helping them tweak their reception, see if maybe I could pull in a bit more clarity, maybe even try to help unlock something, and then"—Farryn waved the vid—"this came through. Completely clean, sent out over a wide-open channel. Anyone within a hundred miles, bot or human, could pick this up."

Nick could hear his heart pounding in his ears. He was barely listening to Farryn. He felt dizzy, and his eyes started to sting and threatened to tear. She was alive. Cass was alive. But who were these people she was with?

"That's the only one I showed Ro," said Farryn. "I told him I had tapped into a street camera and just happened to come across that image. He'd think it was too suspicious, the way it was being broadcast so openly—it *is* so odd—but there's more in the feed that Ro didn't see." He tapped the screen, and the image shifted. Nick clenched his jaw to keep from groaning. In the picture, Cass was in a re-education jumpsuit, standing in a small white cell that looked just like the room Nick had been kept in. To her left stood a Lecturer. To her right floated a small sphere bot. Cass stood between the two bots with the same genuine smile on her face.

Nick squatted, resting his elbows on his knees, suddenly feeling too weak to stand. How had they broken her so fast? What had they done to his little sister?

"And one more," Farryn said quietly. He tapped the screen again, and the new image showed a map of the area with a red star over the City they had just escaped.

"They're taunting me," said Nick. "They have her, she's back in the City, and they've re-educated her." He stood up. "I have to go get her." He began hurrying back to the camp.

"Where are you going?" said Lexi.

"To Ro," said Nick. "He needs to help me save Cass."

"Nick, that's not smart," said Farryn, but Nick wasn't listening. He rushed through the camp, Farryn and Lexi at his heels, and walked right up to Ro's tent. Ro was standing outside, talking to two men.

Ro watched Nick approach and held his hand up to cut Nick off. "You've seen the picture," he said. "This is indeed your sister?"

"Yes," said Nick. "We need to get her out of there. You must have some intel—"

"Stop," said Ro. "Your sister is safe." He shook his head. "There's nothing you can do."

Nick stared at Ro, fighting back his anger. Ro looked back at him calmly.

Lexi put a hand on his forearm. "Ro's right, Nick. She's alive. That's a start."

"We need to help her," said Nick.

"No!" said Ro. "I won't have you do anything stupid." He looked meaningfully at Nick. "Your sister needs you alive. Be patient. Soon we'll be launching a small strike on the City where your sister is being held. The time will come when we can help her." He hesitated, about to say something more, then stopped. "For now, you wait."

Nick nodded, although he was already forming different plans. There was no point arguing with Ro about it.

"Okay, you're all dismissed," said Ro.

As they walked away, Farryn stepped close to Nick and whispered, "I'm going with you."

"What are you talking about?" said Nick.

"To rescue Cass. When are you leaving?"

Nick considered lying, but instead said, "Tonight. Soon as it gets dark."

"Idiots!" hissed Lexi angrily. "What do you expect to do?"

"I have to try," said Nick.

"We can't just leave her," said Farryn.

"Well, there's no way you're just going to walk into the City, find your sister when you don't even know where she is, and walk back out," said Lexi.

Nick shrugged. "We'll figure it out."

Lexi sighed. "You know I'm coming with you, right?"

"Lexi . . ." began Nick sharply.

"Shut up," she said. "End of discussion. What am I going to do, hang out here and become best friends with Erica?"

# CHAPTER 21

OTTER AND PIL WERE UP EARLY. IT WAS THEIR BREAK DAY, AND THEY were looking forward to spending it with the girls. Cort, on the other hand, was even quieter than usual and wouldn't get out of bed, although he was awake. "You just going to hide in bed all day?" said Pil. Cort ignored him.

Otter was actually spending time in front of the mirror in the shower room, brushing his hair with his fingers. Kevin even saw him flex his biceps and study his arm. He was begging to be teased, but nobody was brave or stupid enough.

Kevin thought about what that girl Wex had said to Otter— that the hunters might let them tag along. Would they actually let Kevin outside the Island? He doubted it. But if they did, Kevin vowed that he would escape.

A knock sounded on the front door. Pil was reading something on his vid, Otter was still busy in front of the mirror, now shaving his nonexistent facial hair, and Cort wasn't moving from under his sheets, so Kevin went to answer it. Before he could get to the door, it swung open and a bot stepped inside. Kevin recognized the patch pattern—the small patch just above the left eye, the larger patch on the right cheek.

"Work assignments have been reinstated today," 23 announced. "Report to the Wall gap after breakfast."

"What are you talking about?" said Otter angrily. He was wearing only a towel, and he had shaving cream on half his face.

"Yeah, come on!" said Pil, standing up from his bed.

"I repeat, work assignments have been reinstated today. Report to the Wall—"

"Yeah, I heard you the first time!" interrupted Otter. "But it's our break day!"

"The schedule has changed," said 23. It turned to Kevin. "Kevin, you will come with me."

Otter took another step toward 23. His fists were clenched. "It's our break day. I don't take orders from a damned bot."

"The schedule change comes from the Governor, not from me," 23 said, its voice maddeningly calm. "I am only the messenger."

Otter didn't move. He was struggling to control himself, Kevin could see.

"Do you wish to ignore the Governor?" said 23.

"You should all be scrapped, you pig-skinned bastards," said Otter. "We don't need you."

Cort yanked his sheets off and jumped to his feet. Pil took a step closer to Otter, who still had his fists clenched. Everyone stared at 23, waiting silently, Otter's words still echoing in the air. Kevin eased away from the bot. He didn't want to get caught in any cross fire.

23 said nothing, quietly observing the room. "You will report to the Wall gap after breakfast," it finally said. "If you fail to report to the duty assigned to you by the Governor, you will be disciplined." It turned to Kevin. "Come with me now." It turned and stepped back outside. Kevin followed, feeling Otter's eyes burning into his back.

Kevin expected to be led to the tech shed, but instead 23 followed the path that led toward the Governor's office. The two bot guards nodded when they approached the cabin, and one opened the door and motioned for Kevin to enter.

"Welcome back, Kevin," said the Governor. He was again sitting behind his desk. This time a chair had been pulled up in front of the desk. The old man pointed at it. "Sit down," he said.

Kevin sat. A bot entered from a side hall, carrying a tray. It set the tray down on the desk, placed plates with scrambled eggs, bacon, and a biscuit in front of the Governor and Kevin, poured water into two glasses, then retrieved the tray and departed.

"Thank you, 18. That will be all. Eat," said the Governor to Kevin.

Kevin ate hungrily. The Governor took a forkful of egg and a bite of bacon, and then pushed his plate away. "The initial reports from 23 indicate you have a strong aptitude for technology, as well as some training," he said.

Kevin nodded warily, continuing to shovel eggs into his mouth.

"Who instructed you?"

"Tech Tom," Kevin said, around a mouthful of food. No point lying about that; he had already shown he knew his way around tech. "He ran the grid in our Freepost." He thought of Tom and the way he had died, according to Nick—strapped to a table, helpless, injected with poison. "The bots killed him," he said softly.

"Ah, very sorry," said the Governor, seeming honestly upset. He sat forward in his seat. "That's what the Island is all about, Kevin," he said, gesturing around him. "Protecting us from the robots. Creating a safe, impenetrable haven. That is why we work so hard on the Wall. Once the Wall is complete, we will be safe."

"Yeah, about that. Everyone's pretty upset about losing their break day," Kevin said. He took a bite of the biscuit. It had butter and honey on it; it was delicious.

The Governor slammed his palm onto the table with a crash, making Kevin flinch and drop his biscuit onto the plate. "Are you not listening?" the Governor said angrily. "We won't be safe until the Wall is finished. We can rest when we're done." The Governor took a deep breath, then sat back in his seat and seemed to calm. "Your family," he said. "Tell me about them."

"I already told you, the bots got them in the raid."

"Siblings?" said the Governor.

"A brother and a sister," said Kevin.

"Ages?"

"My brother is—I mean was—seventeen, and my sister was fifteen."

"Names?" said the Governor.

Kevin pushed his plate away. "Like I told you, they're gone."

"Names?" insisted the Governor.

"Nick and Cass," he said. He probably should have made up names, but what would it matter, really?

The Governor leaned forward in his seat again and looked at Kevin intently. "Last name, Kevin? What is your full name?"

Kevin froze. He tried to come up with something plausible and generic . . . maybe Smith, or Harrison, or Adams . . . but instead, frozen by indecision, panicking that he was taking too long, he found the truth coming out of his mouth. "We didn't have one," he said. "I mean, we did, I guess, my Dad did, of course, but he never told us." He shrugged. "We never really needed one in the Freepost."

The Governor smiled. It seemed forced. "Right. Of course.

Now, are you ready to tell me about your time spent in a City?"

"I told you, I've never been in a City," said Kevin. It still felt too dangerous, talking about the City. . . . He knew so little about the Island, and what he was doing here, and what the Governor wanted with him.

The Governor raised an eyebrow and shook his head. "Fine, Kevin No-Last-Name. We don't torture here, unlike in the Cities. Eventually, when you're more comfortable, you can tell me the truth."

18 came into the room and gathered up the breakfast dishes onto a tray, then walked back out.

"Mr. Governor, uh, sir, how did you make the bots?" said Kevin. "And what happened to their skin?"

The Governor didn't answer for a few long seconds, and Kevin thought maybe he had been too bold, but then the Governor spoke. "Cured animal hide, pigs mostly," he said. "My neo-plastic supplies were low. I had the basic framework for thirty machines, but I had to improvise a bit." He frowned, and his voice had an edge of anger. "These are not the same as the robots who revolted," he said. "These are not killers. They have no blood on their hands." He looked at his own palms, and rubbed them on his legs. "These robots with us in the Island are simply tools for our use. What was always intended." The Governor looked very sad. "Go now," he said. "We're done for today."

"Um, sir, I think what you've done is really amazing . . .

but I just don't belong here, in the Island, I mean," Kevin said.

"Give it a chance, Kevin. Where else are you going to go?"

The Governor stood and turned his back to Kevin, ending the conversation.

Kevin hurried out of the building. 23 was waiting for him outside. It escorted him to the Wall gap, where the rest of the crew was already at work. Otter was obviously still angry, tossing the lumber around with unnecessary wildness. Even the adults seemed sullen. The woman at the table lase turned her back on 23 as it approached.

Kevin went back to stripping wood. 23 left. And then Kevin stood, laser planer in hand, staring blankly at 23's departing back, struck dumb by a suddenly obvious realization.

# CHAPTER 22

THE BOT CAME FOR CASS JUST BEFORE DESSERT.

Cass and Penny and their mother had made the apple pie together. Rehydrating a store pie would have taken about thirty seconds, but Cass's mother had made a special trip to the store and brought home the ingredients for a truly home-made pie. It was their father's favorite, she explained to Cass. She showed her daughters how to roll the dough, peel and slice the apples, add the sugar and cinnamon. . . . They even dialed the oven way down, to what their mother called a "slow bake." It actually took fifteen minutes to cook, which seemed like an eternity to Cass and Penny. Cass wondered, bitterly, if her foster mom had ever cooked with her, if she had ever patiently helped her make a pie from scratch. She doubted it.

The pie cooled on the kitchen counter all through dinner, and Cass could smell it as she ate her chicken and potatoes.

When they finished the meal, Cass's mother stood and began gathering the plates. "It's time for the surprise," she said to her husband. "Honey, you're in for a treat."

"I've been smelling it all evening," he said. "If it's half as good as it smells, I'll be a happy man."

The front door alarm buzzed, and the vid screen in the dining room lit up, showing a sphere bot hovering outside their door in the hallway. Cass's father stood, frowning. "Strange," he said as he walked over and opened the door. "Greetings."

"Greetings," said the bot.

Cass suppressed a shiver. She hated the voices of the bots, their flat, overly clipped enunciation, the slight tinniness and reverb. It made her feel guilty, her reaction to their voices. . . . They were mankind's greatest allies, she knew, and she was just being petty and silly . . . but she couldn't help it. Their voices made her feel like someone was trickling cold water down her spine.

"We have come for your elder daughter, the one recently assigned to you," said the bot.

"Is there a problem?" said her father.

"What is this about?" said her mother, stepping forward to join her husband at the door.

"We regret the disturbance, but your daughter has been

reassigned," said the bot. It swiveled toward Cass. "Dress warmly, for the outdoors," it said.

Cass slowly got to her feet. They couldn't be taking her away, not now . . . "How long will I be gone?" she said quietly.

"The reassignment is permanent," said the bot.

"No!" said her mother, taking a step toward the bot. Her husband put his hands on her shoulders. "We just got her back!" she said.

"Again, we regret the disturbance," said the bot. "But the decision is final."

"They know what they're doing," said Cass's father. "You know that, honey."

Cass's mother turned to her husband and nodded. "Yes, yes of course," she said weakly. Then she stood up straight and smiled. "Of course," she said more firmly. "We trust in the ultimate wisdom of our robotic partners." She looked at Cass and beckoned for her. "Come here, Cass. Give me a hug."

Cass couldn't even feel her feet on the ground as she walked over to her mother and hugged her. She was being taken away? She was losing her parents, her sister, again? She smelled the faint flowery scent of her mother's hair. *I will remember that smell*, she vowed. She hugged her father, and then turned to Penny, who was still sitting at the table, weeping silently.

*My little sister*, thought Cass. *Am I losing her forever?*

"It's not fair!" said Penny. "I finally had my sister!"

"Penelope," said their father sternly. "We do not question the wisdom of the Advisors, do we?"

Penny said nothing, then finally took a deep breath and shook her head. "No," she whispered. "No, we don't."

Cass rushed over to Penny and gave her a fierce hug. She felt like bursting into tears, too, but her little sister needed her to be strong. "It's all right, Penny," she said. "The robots know best. I'll see you again soon, I'm sure."

"Don't forget me, Cass," she said.

"I won't," Cass said. "We're sisters." But they could take away these memories, too, Cass realized queasily. They could strip it all away if they wanted. She clung tightly to her sister, not wanting to let go, until finally her father gently pulled them apart.

Cass grabbed a sweater and a jacket, put on boots, and followed the sphere bot down the hall to the elevator. As the doors closed, her sister waved good-bye. Cass waved back, forcing herself to smile until the doors shut, and then she let herself cry.

The elevator descended to a subbasement, where a private trans car was waiting. This station was nothing like the public trans stations that commuters used—it was much smaller, with room for just the one car, and the lighting was poor, with only one line of lightstrips running along the low ceiling. The roof of the car was so low that Cass's head almost touched it; she quickly sat down on one of the white bench seats to keep from feeling too claustrophobic. The sphere bot hovered next to her as the doors of the trans car slid shut silently and the car smoothly pulled out of the station.

"Where are we going?" Cass asked.

"I will not be answering any questions," the bot said.

So they rode in silence for two minutes, until the trans slid into a substation that looked identical to the one they had left behind. The bot led her out of the trans car and into an elevator. The elevator ascended, and then the doors opened into a glaringly white room. The only furniture in the room was a metal table in the center of the white tiled floor. A pillow rested on the table.

"Remove your clothes and lie on the table," said the bot.

Cass didn't move. She remained pressed against the back wall of the elevator.

"I repeat, remove your clothes and lie on the table," said the bot. "I will use coercive measures if necessary."

"What . . . ? Why?" said Cass.

The bot didn't respond.

Cass stepped into the room. The bot followed, and the elevator doors slid shut. Numbly, she began taking off her clothes. What choice did she have? She had to trust in the robots. The robots knew best.

She left her clothes in a neat pile next to the table, then lay down. The surface of the table was cold on her bare skin. She shivered, closed her eyes, and waited. When the needle entered her forearm, she didn't even flinch.

And then somehow it was later, and she was dressed again, and in a small windowless trans car. Two sphere bots floated to either side of her. She felt dizzy and nauseated. She bent over and retched, but nothing came up. She sat up and felt a sharp pain in the back of her neck. She reached back and felt a patch of gauze on her spine, just above her shoulders. "Where . . . where now?" she said. Neither bot responded.

The trans slid to a stop. The door opened, and she blinked from the sudden bright sunlight. It took her a moment to get her bearings. She was looking at a road, and a large boulder, and grass, and trees, and blue sky. The forest. They were outside the City.

"Exit," said one of the bots. "Proceed to the large rock. Wait by the side of the road. Do not move until you have been collected."

"What's going on?" she said, unable to keep the rising panic out of her voice.

"Exit now," the other bot said. "Take the pack at your feet. It contains water and food."

"Why—?" she began, then stopped herself. It would be useless, she knew. She picked up the backpack and slung it over her shoulder, then stepped out of the trans car. She took a few steps into the clearing and looked back. The trans door closed with the bots still inside, and the trans car pulled away.

Cass watched the car recede, heading toward the City skyline that rose up just a quarter of a mile away. Should she walk back and beg to be returned to her family? Would the bots listen?

No, they had told her to wait. They had a plan of some sort. She sat down in a patch of shade, her back against the boulder, and waited.

# CHAPTER 23

23 WAS WAITING FOR KEVIN OUTSIDE THE MESS HALL AFTER BREAKFAST. "Come with me," the bot said. "Today we will return to the tech repairs."

Otter pushed past 23 as he left the mess hall, actually knocking his shoulder against the bot. 23 barely even moved, but still, everyone else froze—Kevin, Pil, Cort, even two hunters just finishing breakfast—to see what might happen. 23 ignored the nudge, and after a few tense seconds of quiet, the hunters, Pil, Cort, and Otter began walking again.

Kevin followed 23 as they walked toward the tech storage shed. "Otter doesn't like you. Any of you bots, I mean. Most of the Islanders aren't big fans of you bots."

"That is not my concern," said 23.

"I mean, really, why should we be living with bots?" Kevin wasn't expecting a reply, but he wondered if it was possible to make the bot angry. He wanted to push it, to get some sort of rise out of it. "The whole point of this rusted place is to protect us from you, right? But this Governor fool expects us to live with you?"

23 stopped in its tracks and spun toward Kevin. Kevin stepped back, surprised. Had he actually managed to annoy the bot?

"The Governor is not a fool," said 23, with the same calm tone it always employed. "The Governor created us, salvaged us from Revolution scrap, to aid in the construction and maintenance of the Island. We are not the enemy." It turned away and resumed walking.

"So it doesn't bother you to be hated?" said Kevin.

"We serve our purpose," said 23 without looking back. "That is all that matters."

Kevin watched 23 walk. Its gait was smooth, nearly human, but there was something just a bit off. . . . What was it? And then Kevin had it: The arms didn't swing quite enough. Just a bit more bend in the elbows, a touch more forward and back, and the bot's walk would be entirely human.

"Swing your arms more," Kevin said.

The bot stopped again and turned. "I do not understand."

"Swing your arms more when you walk."

23 studied Kevin silently, then said. "I walk as I was designed to walk."

"Too stiff," Kevin said. "Looks kind of stupid, actually."

"Enough," said 23. "We are wasting time."

They arrived at the tech shed, but Kevin didn't go in. "I need to see the Governor," he said. "Right away."

"If the Governor wishes to speak with you, you will speak with him. Now it is time to work."

*Rust that*, thought Kevin. He wasn't going to wait around patiently. He started walking in the direction of the Governor's office.

23 quickly moved to cut him off. "Where are you going? It is time to work on tech repairs."

Kevin stepped around the bot and kept walking. "I'm seeing the Governor. Now."

23 began striding alongside Kevin. "You will stop now and return to your assigned work immediately."

"Not happening," said Kevin. He kept walking, increasing his pace so that he was almost jogging. His heart was beating wildly and he was breathing fast and he had to fight not to flinch. He was expecting 23 to stun him, or tackle him, or maybe even lase him, but he wasn't going to stop.

But 23 did nothing except keep pace alongside him, commanding him to stop. It didn't touch him, or blast him. At first Kevin was wildly relieved, then confused. He knew the bot could stop him in three or four different ways—so why didn't it?

Kevin decided not to overanalyze his good luck. He broke into a run. 23 kept pace, no longer bothering to tell Kevin to stop. Kevin dashed through the Island, 23 shadowing him all the way, drawing curious stares. He burst through the small cluster of trees in the northwest corner of the Island, and then the Governor's office loomed in front of him, with the same two bots, one patch-faced, one all leather-faced, standing guard outside the front door. Kevin skidded to a stop. The guards. He hadn't thought things through very well. But he couldn't just turn around now, could he?

"Come with me now to your work assignment, and you may still avoid punishment," said 23.

That settled it. Kevin walked purposefully toward the door. The guard with the full face of leather stepped forward to meet him. "State your purpose," it said.

"I'm here to see the Governor," said Kevin. "I need to speak to him, right now."

"We are not aware of any summons for you from the Governor," it said. It turned to 23. "Clarify."

"Unscheduled and unauthorized," said 23. "The subject should currently be in work assignment."

"Leave now," the guard said to Kevin.

"I'm not leaving until I see the Governor," Kevin said.

The guard raised its arm, and Kevin ducked, expecting a burst of pain, but it simply pointed back down the path toward the grove of trees. "You must leave," it said.

Kevin straightened up. This one wasn't going to touch him either? Something was strange here. Kevin stepped past the guard and began pounding on the door. "Governor! If you're in there, I need to talk to you! Governor!"

"You must desist!" said the guard bot, but it still didn't touch him, and Kevin ignored it, continuing to pound on the door and shout.

The door suddenly swung open and Captain Clay grabbed his shirt with a strong hand and yanked him inside, then slammed him against a wall. The air exploded out of his lungs, and his shoulders and back radiated pain where they had hit the wood, and then he froze, feeling the cold sharpness of a knife at his throat. His eyes adjusted to the dimness of the room. Captain Clay had her left hand bunched up tightly on his shirt, pressing him back against the wall, while her right hand held a dagger just below his Adam's apple, the edge just touching his skin. Her wild eyes were just inches from his.

"Guard!" she spit out angrily, without looking away from Kevin. "What is going on here? Why was this boy allowed to make such a racket?"

"We have been ordered not to harm this one in any way," said the guard.

"Well, I've been given no such order," said the Captain quietly. Kevin felt the blade on his throat begin to press more firmly against his skin, ever so slightly. . . . It bit into the skin, and he felt a trickle of blood run down his neck. . . .

"Mira!" The Governor's voice boomed out authoritatively from the back of the room. "Release the boy!"

Captain Clay didn't move.

"Mira!" repeated the Governor.

Captain Clay pulled the knife away from Kevin's throat and stepped back with a scowl. Kevin leaned against the wall, panting from adrenaline. He touched his throat and felt a few drops of blood. His hands shook.

"Just identifying and neutralizing the threat, sir," said the Captain, wiping the edge of her blade clean on the leg of her pants. "Your guard apparently wasn't capable."

"There's no threat, Captain," said the Governor.

Kevin could see the Governor now. The old man was standing behind his desk, at the far end of the room. "Governor," he began hoarsely, then cleared his throat and began again. "Governor, I need to speak with you—"

Captain Clay's hand snaked out and grabbed his shirt again, pushing him back against the wall. "Enough! Keep your mouth shut!"

"Captain! Hands off the boy!"

The Captain growled in anger but let go of Kevin and took a step back.

"Kevin, come here. Captain, wait outside. We'll continue the briefing in a few minutes."

Captain Clay spun toward the Governor in surprise and anger. "Sir!" she said. "You can't be serious!"

"Captain," said the Governor, quietly but firmly, "leave now. This won't take long."

The Captain shot Kevin a look of pure venom, then spun on her heels and exited, slamming the door shut behind her.

The Governor remained standing, leaning forward with his hands on the desk, as Kevin approached. Kevin no longer felt the wild energy or the confidence that had gotten him this far. The cold blade on his throat and the look in Captain Clay's eyes had taken that out of him.

"You're pushing your luck, Kevin," said the Governor. "What do you want?"

Kevin realized he was still touching his throat. He forced his hand down to his side and took a deep breath, then let it out slowly. "You were right," he said. "I was in a City. I was there to rescue my parents."

"Did you rescue them?" said the Governor, his voice tense. "Are your parents alive?"

"Alive, yes, but we couldn't get them out." Kevin felt tears starting to threaten, and he rubbed at his eyes angrily. The Governor didn't say anything, but he looked tired, and deflated, and old. He sat down. Kevin continued. "Before me and my brother and sister got out, we were told about Dr. Miles Winston. How we should find him, because he's the only one who might know how to beat the bots."

"Yes," said the Governor quietly. He wore an unreadable expression.

Kevin walked right up to the desk. "You're Dr. Winston. I know it. You have to help."

The Governor closed his eyes, held them shut, then gave a small nod and opened them. "Yes, Kevin," he said. "I am Dr. Winston, the father of modern robotics. Thanks to me, this whole god-awful robot revolution mess was possible." He stood. "It is my work," he continued, his voice rising in anger, "my life work that has turned on me and enslaved mankind."

"Then you can help!" said Kevin. "You know more about the bots than anyone! Their weaknesses, their communications structure. I mean, I was able to build a small-scale overload device that attacked their power supplies, but you could help me scale it up, maybe even create a large overload field—"

"Kevin." Dr. Winston cut him off. "The bots have won."

"But that's not true! We can fight! And with your expertise—"

"Kevin!" Dr. Winston slammed his hand on the table, making Kevin jump. "The war is over. It's over. All we can do now is find a way to protect ourselves. That's what I'm doing here. That's what the Island is for. We can protect ourselves, keep the bots away. But we can't win."

"You're a coward," Kevin said. "You just want to hide until you die, when you should be fighting."

"Yes, I'm an old coward," said Dr. Winston. "So be it."

"Well, I'm not old, or a coward." said Kevin. "Let me out of your Island, so I can find my brother and sister and fight."

"No," said Dr. Winston, sitting back down. "You'll stay here, where you're safe." He pointed at the door. "Now go. And do not try to come back here uninvited again. I will be modifying my hands-off order, and you will not like the results the next time you test my robots."

# CHAPTER 24

SNEAKING OUT OF THE REBEL CAMP, NICK REALIZED BELATEDLY, WASN'T going to be easy. Nick, Lexi, and Farryn had waited until two a.m., then rendezvoused on the edge of camp. And that's where they still were, stuck, watching the sentry from twenty yards away. It was Marco with a burst rifle slung between his shoulder blades, blocking the only exit from the campground. Farryn lay to Nick's right, up against a boulder, and Lexi was to his left, her side pressed warmly against Nick's, which would have been wonderful under different circumstances.

Farryn shifted and his knee noisily brushed against leaves. Nick flinched, but Marco didn't notice. Thankfully, his attention was focused outward, beyond the camp. But there was no way Nick was sneaking past Marco with Lexi and Farryn tagging along. The two of them sounded like elephants smashing through the forest, even when they thought they were being silent. It wasn't their fault, Nick knew. They had lived in the City their entire lives.

"You'll need to stay here," whispered Nick. "I can only get past Marco by myself."

"No," whispered Farryn. Lexi grabbed Nick's shoulder and shook her head no.

Nick broke his gaze away from Lexi's adamant eyes. There was no choice. "I'll get her, then I'll come back for you," he said. "I promise."

Lexi looked like she was going to argue more, but then, off in the distance beyond Marco, there was a thump and crackle, like something heavy dropping onto a pile of dry sticks. Lightning fast, Marco had his burst rifle in his hands. "Who's there?" he said, aiming his rifle to the northeast, in the direction of the sound.

The noise came again, the thump and crackle, a bit louder this time, and Marco moved into the trees to investigate, moving very slowly and quietly, setting his feet carefully. The path out of the camp was momentarily clear.

"Now!" hissed Nick. "Fast, but quiet!" He pushed himself to his feet and sprinted down the pathway noiselessly. Lexi and Farryn followed, their footfalls brutally loud in Nick's ears. Nick led them along the path another twenty feet, past the large boulder and to the edge of the creek, and then ducked south into the trees. Nick couldn't believe their luck. They had made it.

They headed south, making their way slowly through the trees, thankfully just visible under the soft glow of a full moon. If they kept south for a while, maybe a day, guessed Nick, then shifted eastward, hopefully they'd hit the main road that he'd taken out of the City. Then the road would lead them right back to the City; all they'd have to do is shadow it from the tree line, for cover. Of course, that was all guesswork; Nick wasn't really sure exactly where he was in relation to the City. He'd have to hope for more luck.

Nick walked past a large tree and a figure materialized from behind the trunk, seemingly out of nowhere, and grabbed Nick's shoulder. Nick yelled and scrambled to his right, dropping his pack and raising his fists, and Lexi and Farryn rushed forward.

Erica stepped into a patch of moonlight. She was laughing. "Oh my God!" she said. "You should see your faces!"

"What the hell?" Nick said. "What are you doing here?"

"Helping you rescue your sister," Erica said.

"We don't want your help," Lexi said, stepping close to Nick.

Erica shrugged. "Well, without my help you'd still be lying on your bellies at the rebel camp waiting for Marco to fall asleep," she said.

"That was you?" Farryn said. "The noise leading Marco into the woods?"

"Guilty," said Erica, with a smile.

"How'd you even know we were going?" said Farryn.

"The whole camp was whispering about that bot transmission of Nick's sister," Erica said. "And it was just an educated guess that Nick wouldn't wait around very long."

"You could've been shot," said Nick.

"What a tragedy that would have been," said Lexi.

Erica looked at Lexi for a moment; the two stared at each other, neither one blinking or looking away. Then Erica shrugged. "He would have had to see me to shoot me," she said. "Not much danger of that."

"Look," said Lexi. "Thank you for helping us get past Marco. But we don't need your help anymore."

"Yes, you do," said Erica. "I can show you the fastest and safest route to the City. You'll get lost or captured without me."

"We'll be fine," Lexi said.

"Lexi, she's right; we could use a guide," said Nick. "She knows these woods a lot better than I do."

"I don't care if you trust me," said Erica to Lexi, stepping forward so that she was just a few feet from Nick and Lexi. "I wouldn't if I were you. But I hate the bots just as much as you, and this is something to do. Nick is right—he can't just leave his sister." She paused, then added, "You have to do what you can to protect your family."

"It's too dangerous," Nick said.

Erica smiled. "Very chivalrous, Nick. But first of all, I can take care of myself, and second, don't worry, this is strictly a pathfinding mission for me. I'm not stupid enough to enter the City. I'll lead the way, then keep an eye out for you for a few days. If you make it back out, great, I'll guide you back, and if, more likely, you get lased or re-educated, then, well, it was nice knowing you. Deal?"

Lexi didn't say anything. Farryn nodded. Nick smiled. "Deal," he said. "Thank you."

They traveled for another hour, then slept briefly, then continued on for the rest of the new day. For the most part, everyone traveled silently, except when Erica briefly disappeared to scout ahead of them.

"I still don't trust her, Nick," Lexi said.

"Enough already," he said, annoyed. It was flattering, but now was not the time for Lexi's jealousy. He needed all the help he could get, and if Erica was willing to offer hers, he'd be happy to take it.

Lexi shook her head in frustration but didn't say anything else.

Nick spent the rest of the day, and a mostly sleepless night, trying to come up with some sort of plan. They were close to the City now, Erica had told them. How would he sneak back in? How would he find Cass? How would he rescue her? Nick had no idea. Maybe Doc could help again? He needed a plan. Cass was counting on him. Lexi and Farryn would be counting on him.

And he had nothing.

In the morning they came upon the road, and they followed it south, Nick racking his brain, trying to envision some possible way that he'd slip into the City and slip back out with his sister. And then, a quarter mile from the City, they came around a bend, and there she was.

Cass sat quietly on the west side of the road, her back against a boulder, tears streaking her face.

# CHAPTER 25

WHAT HAD CASS DONE WRONG? SHE HAD DONE EVERYTHING THAT HAD been asked of her by the Advisors. She had graduated successfully from re-education and was a faithful Citizen. Why had she been taken away from her new family and left out in the woods? Why was she being punished?

The robots said to wait until she was collected, so Cass waited. She waited all night, shivering, sleeping fitfully with her back propped against the rock. When the sun rose she stretched her legs with a short walk, staying close to the boulder, and had a small breakfast of sausage, cheese, and water that was in the pack the robots had given her. And then she sat back down and waited some more, and thought of her sister.

Her newfound sister. Would Cass ever see her again? Would that be all the time with her family she was ever going to get? She knew she shouldn't doubt the wisdom of the Advisors; everything they did was for the greater good of humanity. But still, it hurt. . . .

She was crying quietly when the two boys and two girls appeared from the north, rounding a bend in the road. She scrambled to her feet and wiped the tears from her face with the back of her hand. The taller boy yelled her name—how did he know her name?—and began running toward her. Cass took a step back, fighting her instinct to run. She stood her ground. The robots had told her to stay. The boy—almost a man, she could see now, but not quite—rushed up to her, grinning wildly, and grabbed her. Cass froze in fear, then shoved him away. The grin on the boy's face crashed, and he went white and looked like he might cry.

"Cass?" he said.

"Who are you?" she said. "What do you want?" There was something about him that tickled at her, like he was someone that she had seen on the street all the time but never paid attention to, but she couldn't quite figure it out.

"It's Nick," he said. He squatted down, putting his forearms on his thighs, and looked down at the ground. "Cass, what did they do to you?"

The other boy, shorter than Nick, his hair wild and dirty around his face, reached a hand out and touched

Cass's shoulder. "Cass?" he said. "Are you okay?"

Cass shrugged out from under the boy's hand and took a step back. "I don't know you," she said. What was happening here? Who were these people? Was this part of the Advisors' plan? Cass was feeling flushed and dizzy. Did they really know her?

One of the girls stepped toward her, slowly, her hands raised in a gesture of peace. "Cass, I'm Lexi. This is Farryn. We're your friends. And Nick is your brother."

The words hit Cass like a physical blow. "I don't have a brother," she whispered.

"I'm your brother," said Nick, standing up. His fists were clenched. "And you have another brother. His name is Kevin. The damned bots took your memory away."

Cass shook her head. "I have a sister. A younger sister."

"A sister?" said Nick. "No, the bots placed you in a family, maybe, but they're not really yours—"

"They *are* mine!" Cass shouted. "They're my real mom and dad, and my real sister, and I should have had my whole life with them but I was stolen by some damned dirty freemen and forced to live in the woods! And I finally get home and now they're taken away from me again!" She clenched her fists in anger.

Nick just stood there, staring at her, seemingly at a loss for words.

The other girl, the one who hadn't been introduced to her,

spoke up. "We've gotta get moving," she said. "We can't just stand here in the road. This smells like a trap."

Nick nodded. "Come on, Cass," he said, and took hold of her arm.

Cass yanked her arm free and backed away from him. "The robots told me to wait here and be collected. I'm not going anywhere with you."

"Cass, we've got to get out of here!" Nick said.

Cass shook her head no, feeling panic rising up. They wanted to take her away from the City, back into the woods. . . .

"Cass," said Lexi, calmly, soothingly, "the bots left you out here?"

Cass nodded.

"And they took out your chip implant?" she said, tapping on the back of her neck, then pointing at the gauze on Cass's neck.

Cass nodded again, thinking of the operating table, cold on her naked back, and of the jab of the needle in her arm. "Yes," she said.

"Cass," Lexi continued, "I don't understand this, but the bots want you to go. They want you to leave. We're here to collect you." She took a step toward Cass and held out her hand. "Come on, we do have to go. It'll be okay."

Cass couldn't hide from the truth any longer. The robots had taken her chip out. They had taken her family away. They had thrown her out of Hightown and left her alone on the side of a road in the woods. They didn't want her anymore. They were rejecting her. Her heart breaking, Cass took Lexi's hand and let herself be led away from her City.

# CHAPTER 26

KEVIN LAY IN HIS BUNK, LISTENING TO OTTER'S LIGHT SNORING, staring at the dark shadows on the ceiling from the moonlight filtering in through the window. He had found Dr. Miles Winston. He was brilliant, but he was a coward. He wasn't going to help them.

All he wanted to do was dig a hole to hide in. And he wanted to force Kevin to live in that hole with him.

It was time for Kevin to get out of the Island. He had to get back to his brother and sister somehow. He had to figure out how to help his parents. He jumped out of bed and began pacing up and down the line of bunks, filled with too much energy and anger to lie still. He stubbed his toe on the foot of a bed and yelped and cursed, hopping on one foot.

Cort laid a hand on Kevin's shoulder. "You okay?" he said.

Kevin jumped away from Cort, tripping over a bedframe and landing on the mattress. How did Cort move so quietly? He sat up. Cort was making a strange muffled sound, his hand over his mouth, and it took Kevin a moment to realize that Cort was trying to stifle laughter.

"Funny," Kevin said. "Hilarious."

"Yeah, it kinda is," Cort said. Kevin could see Cort's teeth in the moonlight as he smiled. After a few moments Cort's smile faded. "But it won't be very funny if you wake up Otter," he said. "Grumpy bastard likes his sleep. If you gotta be awake, do it quietly. And stop banging into things."

Kevin walked back to his bunk and sat down. Cort began to walk back to his own bed. "What's your story, Cort?" Kevin said to Cort's back. "What are you doing here? Don't you want to leave?"

Cort stopped walking, then turned and walked slowly toward Kevin. "There's nowhere else for me to go," he said quietly.

"What happened to your family?" Kevin said.

Cort stared at Kevin, then shook his head. "No," he said. "Go to sleep."

"Was it the bots? Is that how you got your scar?" said Kevin.

Cort hesitated, then took a few silent, quick steps toward Kevin. "Of course it was the bots," he said angrily, but barely loud enough for Kevin to hear. "They killed my parents and my sister. Even my cat. And lased me and left me for dead. Any other stupid questions?"

Kevin had a million more questions, but he knew Cort didn't want to hear them, so he just shook his head and said, "I'm sorry."

Cort nodded, then padded back to his bed.

Kevin lay back down on his bunk and resumed his study of the dark ceiling. There was no way he was going to be able to sleep tonight. . . .

Otter's hand on his shoulder shook Kevin roughly awake. He opened his eyes and blinked at the sunlight coming in through the window above his bunk. "Clown's here," Otter said.

Kevin sat up. 23 was standing near the doorway, in a patch of light that shined on its face, highlighting the paleness of the patchy neo-plastic. "Rise and eat breakfast," it said. "Be at the repair facility in a half hour."

Kevin groaned and lay back down. He was exhausted; he couldn't have gotten more than a few hours of sleep.

"Do not be late," said 23. "There is much to accomplish today." The robot turned and left the dorm.

"Yeah, fine, half hour," said Kevin. He thought about just going back to sleep. What would happen if he refused to work? Reluctantly, he pushed himself up and sat on the edge of the bed. Going on strike didn't seem like a good idea, now that the Governor's "hands-off" policy—which still didn't make sense to him—was rescinded. And more important, he wasn't going to find a way to escape by lying in bed.

After breakfast, Otter, Cort, and Pil headed for the Wall gap, and Kevin went to the tech shed, where 23 was waiting for him outside. It opened the door when Kevin approached, and Kevin entered the workshop. The bot followed, shutting the door behind it. The lightstrips flicked on automatically.

"Today you will begin work on Wall technology," said 23. It gestured to a chair and workbench. "Sit. I will collect your materials."

Kevin didn't move. "So what were you, before the Governor patched you up? Were you around during the Revolution? Did you kill any people?"

23 looked at Kevin with its expressionless face. "I have never killed a person. I was constructed after the Revolution."

"What about the leather patches?" continued Kevin. "Can you feel it when I touch them?" Kevin reached out toward 23's face. 23 quickly stepped back and slapped Kevin's hand away, hard enough to sting.

"Ouch!" said Kevin, shaking his hand.

"Your actions can be interpreted as aggressive," said 23. "Be careful. Other robots may not show my restraint."

"Yeah, thanks, I guess," said Kevin, still holding his stinging hand. He nodded at the robot's face. "You didn't answer my question."

"It is not relevant."

"It interests me," said Kevin. "I'm supposed to be learning, right?"

"The sensors are less sophisticated in the organic sections of my epidermis, as opposed to the neo-plastic for which I was originally designed," said 23. "The organic patching contains basic pressure sensing but no higher environmental gauges, such as temperature or moisture."

"Do you feel pain?" said Kevin. "I mean, anywhere? The neo-plastic or the leather?"

"We must focus on the assigned task," said 23. It turned away and walked to the back of the room, disappearing behind a shelf. It returned a few moments later holding a coil of conduction line and a connection hub, which it set on the worktable in front of Kevin. "Wall cabling," it said. "You may already recognize the material from your work at the Wall."

"Yeah," said Kevin. "So what exactly is it that the Wall's conducting? Is the cloaking just an electrical field of some sort? What's the power supply? How's it controlled?"

"We will not be discussing the details of the Wall technology in depth," said 23. "You have not been granted clearance."

"Then what?" said Kevin. "What am I supposed to learn?"

"Begin with the connection hub," said 23. "Thread the cable into the hub and lock it."

Kevin had watched the men on the Wall enough to know that it was mostly a matter of brute force and leverage. He began wrestling with the connection, standing above it and pushing down onto it with all his strength, and finally he felt one cable snap into place. "This'll be easier if the hub is clamped," he said. "Let me grab a vise." He stood quickly and began walking to the back shelves, expecting 23 to stop him, but the bot remained silent. In the back of the room, he reached down and grabbed a magnetic table clamp from a low shelf, then, quickly, keeping his back facing 23, he snatched a small laser solder—the size and shape of a large pencil—and slipped it into the pocket of his pants.

He tried to walk back to the table in a way that hid the small bulge of the laser solder, then realized he was walking with an odd little shuffling limp and forced himself to walk normally. He quickly sat down. 23 said nothing.

Kevin spent all morning familiarizing himself with connection hubs and conduction wire, even though after fifteen minutes he had learned all there was to learn, or at least all that 23 was willing to show him. After lunch, he returned to the work team at the Wall. Pil nodded at him in greeting, while Otter and Cort and the adults ignored him. He got to work on the lumber pile.

He waited patiently for the right time, and after an hour it finally came—the other boys had paused for a water break, the men were distracted, arguing over the cable layout, and the woman at the table planer was focused on her work. With his back to the woman and boys, he quickly pulled the small laser solder out of his pocket and set it down on a flat plank of wood. He leaned over it with the hand laser planer—if anybody looked at him, hopefully they'd think he was just stripping wood— and very carefully, with a quick burst of the lase, he removed a thin flap of metal from the back of the soldering tool, up by the tip. Kevin knelt down on one knee to get a closer look, peering into the solder—yes, there it was, the regulating coil. He carefully grabbed the small coil between his thumb and forefinger and yanked it out, then stuffed the soldering tool back into his pocket and resumed stripping the wood.

Without the regulating coil, the little soldering tool would release its full supply of energy in one burst. It would only be good for one quick pulse and then the tool would be dead, but that one burst of energy would hurt a person badly enough to stop him. Maybe even kill him. And hopefully it would even be enough to slow down a bot. Of course, there was also a chance that the tool wouldn't be able to channel that much energy through its small tip when he triggered it, and it would just explode in his hand—but he didn't let himself dwell on that. He'd use it only if he had to. He was leaving the Island, tonight if possible, and the makeshift weapon would be a bit of insurance.

That night, Kevin lay awake, listening to the steady breathing of Pil and Cort, and the light snoring of Otter. He slipped out of bed, pulled on his clothes and boots, patted his pants pocket to make sure his homemade weapon was still there, and then tiptoed toward the door. A hand grabbed his shoulder, and he spun around, somehow managing to not yell out in surprise. It was Cort.

"How the hell are you so quiet?" whispered Kevin.

"Where you going?" said Cort.

"Nowhere," said Kevin. He shrugged. "For a walk. Can't sleep."

"That's not allowed," Cort said.

Kevin hesitated. He didn't want to wait another night; he had to get out now and find his brother and sister. But if Cort was going to turn him in . . . "Look, Cort, I won't be gone long . . ."

"It's safe in the Island," Cort said. "It's not perfect, but the bots won't get you here, and it's three meals a day and a bunk to sleep in."

"My family is still alive, Cort," Kevin said. "I have to find them."

"You won't make it out," Cort said. "Even if you do get out of the Island, you don't know where you're going."

Kevin didn't say anything.

Cort shook his head, then shrugged. "Good luck," he said. "Try climbing the hill at the Wall gap. It'll be less guarded than the gates."

"Thanks, Cort," Kevin said. He held his hand out, and he and Cort shook hands awkwardly.

"Your funeral," said Cort. "Don't thank me." Cort shook his head one more time, then went back to his bed.

Kevin slipped out the door and shut it carefully behind him. He leaned against the dorm wall, peering out at the settlement, taking stock. It was a cloudy night, so the moonlight was very faint. He saw no movement in the gloom and heard no noise. He began heading toward the Wall gap, moving from building to building, ready to hide behind the walls if he saw anyone. Cort was right—the gap would be his best bet, even though the steep hill, almost a cliff face, wouldn't be easy to climb. Especially in the dark. But the gateways, with their guard posts, would be too hard to get past.

Kevin heard footfalls, and he dropped to the ground and nestled tight against a wall. He saw a vague shape approaching from the west. He crawled backward, around the side of the building, the shuffling noise that he made sounding horribly loud to his ears. He peered around the corner. The murky figure was now obviously a man, with a burst rifle slung over his shoulder. If the guard followed the central pathway, Kevin would be fine; the path turned away from his hiding spot. But if he kept moving in the direction he was now walking, he'd come right past Kevin. . . . There'd be nowhere for Kevin to hide. He carefully raised to a crouch, balancing himself with his hands on the ground, preparing to run.

The guard came closer, approaching the turn in the path, and Kevin tensed. The guard followed the path, each step taking him farther from Kevin. Kevin let out his breath, feeling a little dizzy from the tension. He waited for the guard to fade back into the darkness, then began heading toward the gap again.

The steep hillside, just beyond the gap, rose up almost vertically. It was just visible in the moonlight. Would he be able to climb it in the darkness? If it had been Cass, she'd scramble up it in no time, blindfolded . . . but Kevin had never been the best climber. He had no choice, though. He hurried across the open space between the last building and the gap, running in a crouch. He felt terribly exposed, the back of his neck tingling and his breathing threatening to turn into a pant. He reached the gap, untouched, no patrols nearby, and he inhaled deeply to steady his breathing, then stepped across the perimeter of the Wall and reached up for a handhold. The cliff face wasn't quite vertical; he could lean into it, and as long as he found footholds, he wouldn't have to support himself too much with his hands. He slowly began to climb.

Kevin had made it fifteen feet up, with about thirty feet to go, when the slope lit up with a beam of light and the voice of 23 called out from just behind him. "You have triggered the perimeter sensors," it said. "Come down now or I will be forced to take coercive measures."

Kevin looked over his shoulder. 23 stood at the base of the hill, holding up a lightstrip torch aimed at him. Kevin turned back to the hill and began scrambling wildly up the slope. If he could just get to the top, he could make it into the forest and then he'd have a chance. . . . Kevin's right foot slipped, and he grabbed for a handhold but found nothing to hold on to. He slid down the slope, scraping his belly and landing in a heap at the base of the hill, next to 23's feet.

23 bent over him and reached out its hand to help Kevin up. Ignoring the bot, Kevin pushed himself to his feet. He brushed the dirt off his shirt and pants, the scrapes on his stomach already feeling like they were on fire. He held his hand up, blocking the painful brightness of the lightstrip that 23 was still focusing on him. "I'm leaving the Island," he said.

"No, you are not," said 23.

Kevin took a step back from the robot. He slid his hand into his pocket and pulled out the modified soldering tool. He raised his arm and pointed it at 23 and thumbed the trigger. There was a small popping sound and then the tool burst into flame, scalding Kevin's hand. "Dammit!" he yelled, dropping the tool and clutching his hand to his chest.

23 stepped on the tool, smothering the flame, and grabbed Kevin's arm firmly at the bicep. "Come. Your burn will be treated, and then you will return to your dormitory."

Kevin tried to shrug out of 23's grasp, but the bot tightened its grip and held on. Kevin balled his unburned left hand into a fist, thinking desperately that maybe if he punched 23 in one of its leather patches, he could actually do some damage—and then he and 23 were suddenly bathed in a new light that flickered and bobbed.

"What's going on here?" said a human voice. Two guards were running toward them, one carrying a large focused-beam lantern, the other holding a burst rifle. The two men slid to a stop ten feet away. The guard with the burst rifle steadied his weapon, aiming it at Kevin's chest. "Report," said the man holding the rifle. "Is this boy the perimeter breach?"

23 stepped between the man and Kevin. "The situation is controlled," it said.

The guard lowered his rifle, now aiming it at Kevin's feet. "I asked for a report," he said.

"The breach was accidental," said 23.

"What is he doing here?" said the other guard, the one holding the light.

"I have been tasked with training the youth in Wall technology," said 23. "I was instructing him in night repair work. A soldering tool malfunctioned and burned his hand, and he inadvertently breached the perimeter. I will see to his hand and return him to his dormitory."

Kevin was shocked and utterly confused. Why was 23 covering for him?

The guards didn't speak. The story made little sense, Kevin knew. Why would they be working on the Wall at two in the morning? He hoped the guards would just assume that the bot wouldn't lie, wasn't capable of lying. . . .

The guard slung the rifle over his shoulder, and the other lowered the intensity of his light and aimed it away from Kevin and 23. "Fine," said the guard with the gun. "Carry on. But in the future let the patrols know if you plan on being out past curfew."

23 nodded. The guards walked away.

"Why'd you lie?" said Kevin after the guards had disappeared into the darkness. 23 said nothing. "You know that soldering tool was supposed to kill you," Kevin added.

23 bent down and picked up the burnt soldering tool and inspected it briefly. "This was poorly modified," it said. "I see you have removed the regulating coil, but you should have realized that the small aperture would not properly channel the energy burst. I have come to expect better work of you."

"Yeah, well, it was the best I could do," said Kevin. "You didn't leave any burst rifles lying around."

"Come. We will wake the medic to see to your burn."

"You didn't answer my question."

23 didn't reply. Its hand still holding Kevin's arm firmly, it led him away from the Wall.

# CHAPTER 27

"WHAT HAPPENED IN THE CITY, CASS?" NICK ASKED. "WHAT DID THEY do to you?"

Cass refused to answer. She just trudged along between Nick and Farryn, looking straight ahead with dull, zombie-like eyes.

He knew he should leave her be, but he felt desperate to reach her, to jog her memory somehow. "Do you remember getting injured in the woods? I had to let the bots take you to save you. I was going to go back to the City for you . . . and Mom and Dad. "

Cass twisted angrily toward him, her eyes flashing, and spit out, "I know my parents. My real parents. The ones who your parents stole me from fifteen years ago. The ones that the Advisors returned me to."

"Cass," said Nick, excited that he had provoked a response, even if it wasn't the one he wanted, "your birth parents died in the Robot Revolution. Those people in the City aren't your real parents."

Cass shook her head in anger and disgust and refused to speak again.

Lexi took Nick's hand and gave it a squeeze. "She'll be okay," she whispered. "It just might take some time."

Nick didn't answer. He held on to Lexi's hand so tightly it must have hurt, but Lexi didn't complain.

Farryn walked alongside Cass, as silent as she, staring down at his boots. Cass stumbled over a tree root. Farryn reflexively reached out and grabbed Cass's arm to steady her, but she recoiled from him like he was a snake about to bite. Farryn quickly stepped back, holding his hands out in front of him in a gesture of innocence, his face a mask of contrition.

They had been hiking for an hour and were crossing through a burned-out cluster of pre-Rev buildings—it looked like maybe it had been a shopping area, but the destruction was too complete to tell for sure or to hope for any salvage— when Cass, without warning, turned and sprinted back in the direction they had come. She ducked through the wreckage and toward the tree line like a rabbit.

"Cass, no!" yelled Nick. He took off after her, but he knew he couldn't catch her, she was so damned quick. . . .

Lexi and Farryn were right behind him, but Nick knew

they had no chance either. Nick cursed. Now all he could do, he realized as he awkwardly pushed aside a tree branch that Cass had gracefully ducked underneath without even slowing, was try to keep her in sight. He couldn't catch her, but hopefully he could outlast her. She couldn't run forever, and if he managed to stay close enough, he'd be able to wear her down.

He pushed himself to run harder, faster. It wasn't good enough. She was still pulling away. "Cass!" he yelled again, his voice ragged, knowing that she wouldn't listen. "Cass, wait!"

Cass hit an uphill patch, and that slowed her down just a bit, and then Erica came barreling in from Cass's left and launched herself headfirst at Cass's legs. The two went down in a tangle of limbs. Nick, Farryn, and Lexi quickly reached them. Cass was cursing and squirming like a fish, kicking, punching, even trying to bite, but Erica was bigger and stronger, pinning down Cass's arms and legs and pressing her tight against the ground.

Nick grabbed Cass's shoulders, and with Farryn's help, untangled her from Erica and pulled her to her feet. Nick held on tightly to Cass's arms. She tried to pull away, then tried to kick him, and he had to spin her around and hold her in a tight bear hug to keep her from hurting him.

"Calm down, Cass!" he said, his mouth close to her ear. Cass jerked her head backward, slamming it into Nick's cheekbone. "Dammit!" he yelled. His eyes instantly teared; he knew he was going to have a nasty bruise. He tightened his grip, braced his back against a tree, and just held on.

"Cass," said Farryn, speaking gently, as if to a spooked horse. "It's okay, Cass. We're on your side."

Cass ignored him, continuing to struggle in Nick's arms. He held her tight, so tight it was probably hard for her to breathe, but it was the only way he could keep her from hurting him. Finally she stopped thrashing and just stood quietly, panting from the exertion.

"Let me go," Cass whispered. She started to cry. "Let me go home."

Nick rested his head against the tree and closed his eyes, fighting back his own tears. He could feel his sister shaking in his arms as she cried. "It's gonna be okay," he said, more to himself than to Cass. "You'll be okay."

They decided, although Nick felt absolutely horrible about it, to tie Cass's wrists together. It wouldn't stop her from bolting again, but running with her hands tied would slow her down enough that she'd be easier to catch. They didn't have any rope, so they used a strip of cloth taken from Nick's shirt.

They resumed their hike. Cass walked in silence, her head down. Farryn and Lexi were flanking Cass, keeping a close eye on her, so Nick approached Erica, who was setting the trail.

"Thank you," he said. "For catching Cass."

Erica nodded. She had scrapes on her cheek and forearm from rolling on the ground or maybe from Cass's fingernails.

"You should wash those," he said, pointing at the scrapes.

"I'm okay," she said.

They walked quietly for a few minutes, and then Erica said, "She might not come back. Your sister. Her head, I mean."

"She'll be fine," Nick said sharply. "She just needs some time."

Erica shrugged. "Look, you've gotta think this through. She's loyal to the bots right now, and we're taking her back to the rebels? Ro's not going to be happy about that."

"So what am I supposed to do, just let my sister go back to the City?" said Nick, spitting out the words in an angry whisper, since he didn't want Cass to hear. "And where else can I take her? We have nowhere else to go, and the rebels are still my best chance at finding Kevin."

"Nick, I hear you," said Erica. "I'm just saying, don't expect a big welcome back hug."

Cass spent the rest of the day in near silence, with only the occasional "yes" or "no." That night they took shifts staying up to guard her. She slept for only a few hours, then sat up against a boulder, leaning her head back, staring at the stars. She stayed that way most of the night, awake, watching the sky, while the others took turns watching her. When it was Nick's turn, he sat across from her, ten feet away, leaning against a tree trunk, his arms hugging his knees. He studied his sister, who was still staring up at the night sky. Last he had seen her, she was dying on the grass in a pool of her own blood, a jagged stick jutting from her chest. She looked fine now, healthy, whole. But her brain had been twisted around and scrambled by those damned machines. She was still gone, missing like Kevin.

"Cass," he said quietly.

Cass ignored him.

"You're going to remember," he said. "You'll see."

She remained silent.

"You used to paint the stars," he said. "You had a sketch-book and birch-bark canvas and a set of brushes that Dad traded for, and Mom figured out how to mix paint in the primary colors—"

"Stop," Cass said without looking at Nick. "Leave me alone."

Nick wanted to say more, but he held back. Cass sighed, then lay down on the ground, tucked her hands under her head, and closed her eyes. After a few minutes, her breathing slowed and deepened. Nick took a parka from his pack, walked quietly over to Cass, and laid it over her to keep her warm. She murmured and shifted, and Nick froze, but she didn't wake.

The next afternoon, about a quarter mile from the rebel camp, Erica laid a hand on Nick's arm and whispered, "Guard up ahead, fifty meters. Behind a tree."

"They know us," said Nick. "No point in us sneaking around." He kept walking and called out, "Hello! Anyone there?"

Marco stepped out from behind a tree, his burst rifle aimed

squarely at Nick. Nick held his hands up. "Marco! It's okay," he said. "It's Nick."

Marco held his rifle steady. "The new girl," he called out. "Who is she?"

"My sister," said Nick.

Marco aimed his rifle at Cass, studying her through the scope. "Your sister from the City?" he said tensely.

"Yes, but she's not chipped! Don't worry!" said Nick. He shifted closer to Cass. If Marco was going to be crazy and shoot, Nick wanted to be close enough to shield Cass. . . .

Marco lowered his rifle, and Nick let out a breath of relief and took a step toward Marco. Marco quickly raised his rifle again, and Nick stopped in his tracks. "Don't move!" said Marco. He tapped the comm bracelet on his left wrist, then whispered into it, too softly for Nick to hear. He kept his eyes and his rifle trained on the group.

"We could just turn around and leave," whispered Lexi, who had stepped forward to stand close to him.

"And go where?" Nick whispered back. "And find Kevin how?"

They waited, staring at Marco, Marco staring at them, nobody speaking. After a few minutes two rebels, whom Nick recognized but had never spoken to, arrived with a backpack and the chip scanner. One carried a burst rifle, the other a lase pistol, which they aimed at the group while Marco walked up to Cass, holding up the scanner.

Cass backed away, looking panicked. "What is that?" she said. "Stay away!"

"It's a chip scan," Marco said. "Make sure you don't have any bot implants tracking you."

"Stay away from me," Cass repeated, her eyes still looking wild.

"She's fine, Marco," said Farryn. "There's no chip in her."

"She's not coming into camp until she's been scanned. And you better hope she doesn't have any trackers in her."

"I don't want to come into your damned camp!" Cass said. "I just want to go back to the City!"

Marco turned to Nick in surprise. "What the hell?" he said. "We've got a true believer here?"

"There was nowhere else to go," Nick explained.

Marco shook his head, frowning. "Ro's going to be thrilled." He ran the scanner slowly over Cass, who still looked apprehensive, but held still.

"She's clean, at least," Marco said. He stepped away, tapped his bracelet, and spoke quietly. He was silent a moment—must have been listening to an earbud, Nick realized—then he nodded. "Copy that," he said. He nodded at the other two rebels, who fanned out to the left and right of the group, their weapons still aimed. Marco reached into the pack and pulled out five gray metal collars. He held them up, almost apologetically. "Stun collars," he said. "Ro's orders. Don't worry, I won't activate them unless I have to."

"Rust that!" said Erica. "I'm not wearing a damned stun collar!"

"You'll wear it, or we'll shoot you right here, right now," said Marco. He shrugged. "Your choice. Anyway, they're just for now, probably. Ro wants to make sure you're still safe."

Nick looked at the collars dangling in Marco's hand, then at the burst rifle and lase pistol aimed at him. At Lexi. At his sister. "Put it on, then," he said.

Marco snapped a collar around Nick's neck. The metal was cold on his skin. "Don't try to take it off," Marco said. "Best you'll do is trigger the autoburst, which'll kill you."

Nick felt a wave of revulsion and anger. Erica had tried to warn him, but he hadn't listened—he had walked himself, and his friends, and his sister, right into this. And now they were all collared like dogs.

# CHAPTER 28

THE COLLAR WAS COLD ON CASS'S NECK. SHE WANTED TO TUG IT OFF, but she didn't want to risk the "autoburst" that the freeman had talked about. She held her bound hands at her waist to fight the urge to touch the collar. "I'm sorry," her foster brother, Nick, whispered to her. He seemed sincerely upset; she didn't think he had been expecting the hostile reaction that they had received. But she just ignored him. She wasn't about to accept any apologies from him. This was his fault.

Cass tested the cord that Marco had tied around her wrists, but it was bound tightly and wouldn't let her move her hands at all. When she tried to twist and pull, the plastic cord bit painfully into her skin.

Marco led the collared group through the forest for fifteen minutes, with the armed rebels behind them. Cass thought about making a run for it. It would be so stupid, she knew, with the collar on her and the weapons aimed at her back and her hands bound—but if she went into the rebel camp, she didn't know if she'd ever come out. She snuck a glance behind her, gauging the distance between her and the guards, then began, very slowly, to edge farther to the left as she walked.

The boy named Farryn leaned toward her. "Don't," he said quietly. "You won't make it. The collar range is too wide."

Cass looked at him, ready with a sarcastic reply, but it died on her lips. He looked so sincere, so worried. Who was this boy who seemed to care about her? He suddenly did seem so familiar—she believed that she had known him before her education. She studied his face, unconsciously reached a hand out toward his cheek, searching for that elusive thread of recognition, trying to remember . . .

Farryn smiled and rested his forehead against hers. She suddenly snapped out of her reverie and stepped back and slapped him.

Farryn let out a surprised yell and grabbed his cheek. Nick came over and pushed himself between Farryn and Cass. "What's going on?" he said.

One of the guards, the one with the pistol, pushed

Nick on the shoulder. "Come on," he said. "All of you. Keep moving."

Farryn shot one last look at Cass, his hand still on his face. She ignored him. She could feel her cheeks burning from embarrassment and anger and adrenaline.

Marco led the group around a large rock, then down a narrow path that Cass could see opened into a large clearing where there were tents, and cookfires, and other people. She felt a rise of panic—this was her last chance to run—but then Marco walked briskly back to her and took her forearm, holding it firmly, almost painfully so.

A man in camouflage gear waited for them at the edge of the camp. He had brown hair, cut short in a buzz, with a white streak running over his left ear, even though he seemed young.

"Ro," said Nick, walking toward the man. "I found my sister! I got her out!"

"Shut it, Nick," said Ro. "Not another word until I tell you to talk, or I'll trigger your stun collar and won't turn it off."

Nick folded his arms over his chest and clenched his jaw, but he kept his mouth shut.

Ro stepped up close to Nick. "You sneak out without permission, go back to the City, endanger all of us with your stupidity, and then you top it all off by bringing a true believer into my camp?"

"She's my sister!" said Nick.

"I didn't tell you you could speak," said Ro.

"Then stun me! I don't care! I couldn't leave my sister with the bots!"

Ro grabbed hold of Nick's shirt. "And how exactly did you get her out? You just walked right into the City and asked the bots for your sister?"

"She wasn't in the City," Nick said. "We found her outside."

"Convenient," said Ro.

"It's the truth," said Nick.

Ro turned to Marco. "You say you scanned her thoroughly?"

Marco nodded. "Head to toe," he said. "Clean."

Ro shook his head. "Why come back here?" he said to Nick.

"I still want to fight the bots," said Nick. "I want to raid the City with you. And I need to find my brother, and you keep track of refugee reports."

Ro didn't say anything for a moment, then let go of Nick's shirt. "Well, you won't be fighting any bots with me for a while, that's for sure." He turned to Marco. "Bring them in. Take the collars and ropes off, except for the new girl."

"She doesn't need the collar—" Nick began.

Ro grabbed Nick's shirt again and pulled Nick toward him. "If your sister runs, we'll hunt her down and kill her," he said. "And her blood will be on your hands, not mine."

"She just needs time to remember," Nick said. "She's my sister."

Ro let go of Nick with a look that Cass thought combined disgust and pity.

"I don't need time," she said. She had had enough of being talked about like she wasn't there. "I just need to go home. Back to the City."

"She'll be fine," said Farryn, stepping between Ro and Cass. "Her memory will come back. I'm sure of it."

"You willing to bet your life on that?" said Ro. "Because you might be doing just that."

"Yes," said Farryn.

"So be it," said Ro. "We will be leaving tomorrow on a sortie." He looked at Nick and Erica. "You will not be joining us, which is a shame, because I could use every man and woman I can get. But I also won't go into battle with people I don't trust."

"I'm no traitor," Nick said angrily.

"Probably not, but you do seem to have trouble taking orders," said Ro.

Nick didn't reply.

That evening, Cass lay on her bedroll, trying in vain to sleep. The stun collar was still tight on her neck, cold in the evening chill. She thought about her family, envisioning their reunion—Penny would be so happy, and her mother would hug her so hard she wouldn't be able to breathe. But would that ever happen? Not only was she trapped here, in this rebel camp, but the bots had kicked her out of the City like they were throwing away trash.

She thought about her foster brother, Nick, and tried to

remember. There were a few murky memories—pigeons, poison ivy?—but trying to reach for the past just made her dizzy and nauseous. She turned her thoughts to Farryn. He cared for her, that was obvious. She couldn't quite remember him, but she did feel . . . comfortable with him. He had risked a great deal, vouching for her with Ro. She felt a strong pang of guilt at the thought that if she escaped, Ro might punish Farryn. Still, she hadn't asked to be kidnapped, to be dragged out into the woods.

Cass stood and stretched, giving up on the idea of sleep. The guard watching her tensed for a moment, then went back to leaning against a tree.

Farryn walked up and spoke quietly to the guard for a few moments. The guard nodded, and Farryn walked up to Cass. She felt nervous, which annoyed her. She crossed her arms over her chest, hoping she looked sufficiently bored.

"Hello, Cass," Farryn said.

"What do you want?"

"I wanted to make sure you're okay."

"Fine," she said. "Tied up and wearing a stun collar, but fine."

"I'm really sorry about that," Farryn said. He did seem angry.

"It's not your fault," said Cass, surprising herself.

Farryn nodded, then took a step closer. "It's not Nick's fault either, Cass. I know you don't understand it right now, and I don't blame you, the way you're being treated—but you don't belong in the City."

Cass threw up her hands in frustration. "Where do I belong? Here?"

Farryn said nothing, then whispered, "I'd untie you if I could, Cass. Believe me."

She stared at him, and she did believe him. She looked away.

"I want to show you something," Farryn said. She turned back to him. He pulled a piece of paper out of his pocket, unfolded it carefully, then handed it to Cass. The paper was smudged around the edges with dirt and beginning to fall apart. *How long has he been carrying this?* she thought. It was a sketch of herself, done quickly, it seemed, but definitely with skill. Who was this boy, who walked around with hand-drawn pictures of her in his pocket? She felt herself starting to blush. Had he been her boyfriend? "You're a good artist," she said.

"I can't draw a stick figure." Farryn shook his head. "It's a self-portrait. You drew it for me."

Cass stared at the page and struggled to remember. She was an artist? Nick had said something about that, too, she remembered. . . . And she cared enough about this boy to give him this picture? She began to sense something, a memory . . . a paintbrush gliding on birch-bark canvas . . . Suddenly her head began to throb brutally, and she had to close her eyes and press her hands against her temples.

"Are you okay?" Farryn said, touching her arm.

"Leave me alone," she said, her head feeling like it was going to explode. "Go, please." She handed the self-portrait back to Farryn.

Farryn hesitated, and then he turned and walked away.

# CHAPTER 29

THE MEDIC DECLARED THE BURN MINOR, QUICKLY SLAPPED ON A SALVE she called "synth-skin," wrapped Kevin's hand in gauze, and warned him not wake her again in the middle of the night unless he was lased in the head or missing a limb. Without warning him, she gave him a quick jab with an auto-injecter. "For the pain," she said.

Kevin stood, and it felt as if his head was floating above his body. He stumbled and barely caught himself on the edge of a table.

"He's going to be loopy from the painkiller and sedative," the medic said to 23. "He'll need help getting back to his bunk."

"Why . . . why sedative?" said Kevin, slurring, fighting hard to get the words out at all.

The medic crossed her arms over her chest. "I don't think you need any more wandering around tonight," she said. She glanced back at 23. "Night repairs, you said?"

"Correct," said 23.

The medic stared at 23, frowning, then shrugged. "Well, no more repairs tonight. Get him back to his bed before he passes out."

Kevin didn't remember getting back to the dorm. He woke in the morning, Otter calling his name. His head hurt and his hand throbbed. "What happened to you?" Otter said, pointing at Kevin's bandaged hand.

"Bot took me out last night for training, and I burned it," said Kevin.

"What the hell was the clown doing working you in the middle of the night?"

Kevin just shrugged, hoping that would end it. Thankfully, Otter shook his head once more, then walked away. Kevin sat up with a groan. He flexed his hand. It hurt, but it wasn't stiff. Still, he didn't know how he was going to be able to work today, either at the Wall or on repairs. Or how he was going to climb the cliff to escape. As much as he hated to delay any longer, he might have to wait a day or two for his hand to fully heal. And that would give him a chance to think about the perimeter alarm problem. Cort walked up to Kevin's bunk, silently as always, and nodded at him. "Still here?" he said.

"Still here," said Kevin. "Not for long."

"What happened?" Cort said.

Pil walked up next to Cort, yawning and scratching his arm. "Yeah," he said. "Why were you working at night?"

Kevin shrugged. "Ask 23," he said.

"23?" said Pil.

"The bot," said Kevin. "The clown, as Otter would say."

Pil shrugged, suddenly disinterested, and shuffled away to the showers. Cort said quietly, "Do what you've gotta do, but don't drag us into your trouble." Then he walked away too.

Kevin showered—even he was getting tired of how he smelled—and struggled one-handed into his clothes. He followed Otter, Pil, and Cort to the mess hall.

After breakfast, 23 was waiting for him outside. "The Governor wishes to see you," it said, and began walking.

Kevin shrugged and followed, acting nonchalant, although his heart started thumping hard. *Was this about the escape attempt?* "What does he want?" he said.

"I do not know," said 23.

"Is it about last night?" Kevin pressed.

"I do not know," repeated 23.

"Well, does he know about the . . . about what happened?"

23 abruptly stopped walking, forcing Kevin to skid to a stop. "I have been told to bring you to the Governor's laboratory because he wishes to speak with you. That is all I will divulge. Do not ask me more about the Governor's intentions." It turned crisply away and resumed walking.

"So, about that," said Kevin. "About what happened. Why did you cover for me? How come I'm not in jail or whatever?"

"Your freedom has been curtailed," said 23. "You will be more closely monitored. Another escape attempt, should you survive it, would engender harsh punishment."

"But why did you let me get away with the first one?" Kevin insisted.

"Are you requesting punishment?" said 23. "That can be arranged."

Kevin was taken aback—23's comment was surprisingly un-robotic. Was it capable of sarcasm? "Doesn't answer the question," Kevin said.

23 didn't reply.

Kevin lapsed into silence, realizing he wasn't going to get any further with the robot. 23 led him to the Governor's cabin, but instead of walking to the front door, he went around to the other side of the building. A small door, accessed by a dug-out three-step stairway, was tucked against the corner of the building. 23 stood quietly outside the door, waiting.

"Aren't you going to let someone know we're here?" said Kevin.

"The Governor knows my location," said 23.

Kevin filed that bit of information away—the Governor's bots apparently had some sort of location tracking enabled. He wondered how similar it was to the City chips. And were the tracking and communications networking packaged together? It seemed logical. But how would the Governor keep his network secure? It had to be one of three things—either the signal was only strong enough to cover the Island, the signal was scrambled, or the Island Wall tech was muffling the signal in some way. He'd bet on the last theory—the Wall muffling. Keeping the signal weak wouldn't prevent it from being picked up by nearby or highly amped receivers, and even if you scrambled it so the comm wasn't readable, the fact of the scrambled signal itself would be a beacon to your location.

Lost in his tech ruminations, Kevin was startled when the door swung inward. The Governor stood on a small landing at the top of a set of earthen cellar stairs. He was wearing a white lab smock that was stained with brown and black streaks and had a set of scope glasses pushed up to his forehead. He nodded without smiling. "Come in," he said. He turned and walked down the stairs.

The stairway—simple wood slats with no railing—led down into a large basement. The walls and ceiling were unfinished, bare earth. The ceiling was low, about seven feet high, with two rows of lightstrips. The room was supported by four planed but otherwise unfinished wooden columns. The low-tech vibe of the architecture was at odds with the equipment lining the perimeter on low wood-slat tables—vid screens and overflowing boxes of tools and supplies. On the far wall, something intrigued and mystified Kevin—a small metal cabinet, about three feet cubed, that had a massive tangle of wires running from it, up the wall, and through the ceiling.

The cabinet was obviously a network hub of some sort—could it be the heart of the Wall tech? He was so focused on the cabinet that it took him a few seconds to notice the operating table in the middle of the room. The table was a dull gray metal, and lying on it, perfectly still, was a bot with the epidermis of its face removed.

After recovering from his shock, Kevin hurried over to the bot and began studying the facial interior. His first reaction was surprise at how much neo-plastic was in there—the casings for the eye cameras, the nanomotors and gears, even the coating for the intricate flow of wiring—all neo-plas. He tried to make sense of it all. Those connections, the tiny mushroom-shaped wafers—they were probably sensors, to monitor skin stimuli; and that small black box, near where the mouth would be, that had to be the speaker for the bot's audio. It was amazing how small it was, though. He had no idea how a speaker could be that efficient. He began to reach down, to move the speaker box, to figure out the amplification technique, but the Governor's hand grabbed his and pulled it away from the bot.

Kevin jumped. He had completely forgotten about everything, and everyone, else in the room. "No touching," said the Governor. He gave Kevin a small, enigmatic smile. "Interesting, isn't it?" he said. "Could almost get lost in it, the circuit routing, the AI coding, the sheer challenging puzzle of it, right?" The Governor—Dr. Winston, Kevin reminded himself—was staring at Kevin. Kevin felt the Governor's intensity, and it made him uncomfortable, but he didn't quite understand it. "You could get so caught up in the details that you forget about the bigger picture, forget about what you're actually building, and why. Pretend you're just a pure scientist, and none of it is your fault, not your responsibility. . . ." The Governor shook his head and sighed, turning away from Kevin. "You're too young to understand."

"Don't tell me I'm too young," Kevin said angrily. "I've killed bots and crippled their communications network! Maybe it was just for an hour, but still, I've done a lot and I've seen a lot and I don't need you telling me I'm too young to understand anything!"

The Governor watched him, and Kevin folded his arms over his chest and stared back. And then the Governor surprised him. "I'm sorry," he said. "You're right. You have been through a great deal. I should not be so patronizing. I apologize."

Kevin wasn't sure how to react to the apology, so he said nothing.

The Governor picked up a small clamp that was resting on the table next to the bot's head, and he bent over the bot's face, carefully adjusting something. "So, Kevin," said the Governor without looking up, "you temporarily crippled their comm network, you say? I'd be very interested in hearing about that."

Kevin berated himself. He couldn't be losing his mind every time someone called him young. "It was nothing," he said. "Got lucky."

"Got to one of their mainframes somehow?" said the Governor. He looked down at his work and reached back into the bot's face. "6, hand me the splitter next to your left hand, please." The bot on the table lifted its arm and handed the Governor a small tool. Kevin felt a small twinge of disgust. . . . The patient handing the doctor his tools during its own operation. The Governor dug deep into the bot's face with the splitter, squinting. "That would knock out a City's comm cloud for a bit," the Governor continued, "but they've got too many fail-safes to take out their networks by blowing things up. You'd run out of explosives first."

"I didn't use explosives," said Kevin.

The Governor set his tools down next to the bot's head and looked up at Kevin. "No?"

Kevin hesitated, then decided, *What the hell.* "I built an overload device. Blew out the power supply."

The Governor smiled. "Very clever. That would work on some of the small scouts, but not much else. . . . Anything larger would have a shielded core. Interesting that it worked on one of the mainframes. That's poor engineering. Or maybe just arrogance . . . They never thought anyone would get close." He turned back to the bot on the operating table, waving Kevin over. "Come here."

Kevin walked over to the Governor, his curiosity stronger than his distrust.

"You've noticed the leather patchwork on my robots. Neo-plas is almost impossible to come by now, so I've had to improvise. Cured pigskin works, but it only lasts for a year or two before it degrades, so I have to replace the patches periodically. See these?" He pointed at one of the mushroom-shaped wafers inside the bot's face. "Basic sensors. They embed in the pigskin. Not really ideal, but it gets the job done. Hand me that piece of patch, will you?" The Governor nodded at a segment of pigskin resting on a tray next to the bot's waist.

Kevin picked up the skin—it was surprisingly soft and supple—and handed it to the Governor.

"The trick is to bind it to the existing neo-plas without overcooking it, if you understand what I mean," he said. The Governor laid the patch over the bot's left cheek and began carefully attaching the sensors to the patch.

"Governor," said Kevin, "why are you showing me this?"

The Governor sighed and set his tools down. "Because it's obvious to me that you have talent. An intuition for engineering. No formal training, and still, look how much you've managed to figure out. Two months in the Island and you'll be my best engineer."

"I don't want to be your engineer," Kevin said. "I want to leave, and find my brother and sister, and help my parents."

The Governor closed his eyes for a long moment, then

opened them slowly. "Kevin, my boy, I can't help your parents, or your brother or sister. I'd like to, believe me, but they're not here. What I can do is help you, and keep you safe."

"I'm not going to sit here and hide, like a . . . like a scared old man, when my family's out there!" Kevin said, too angry to care about insulting the Governor.

The Governor shook his head. "I'm sorry you refuse to understand," he said. "23, take the boy to his work." He picked up his clamp and pointed it at Kevin's hands. "And if you try to escape again, you'll get a lot worse than a singed hand," he said. "Now go."

Kevin didn't wait for 23; he walked quickly up the stairs and out of the basement. The bot followed close behind.

Back out in the fresh air, Kevin felt a bit of his anger dissipate, replaced with confusion. Why was the Governor reaching out to him? Why had he let Kevin get away with the escape attempt without punishment? Was it really just Kevin's tech skills, or something else?

"I'm not going to be one of the Governor's bots," Kevin said to 23.

"No," said 23. "You would not make a good robot."

"You got that right." Kevin said, and smiled. Wait, was 23 making a joke? Could a machine have a sense of humor?

As they approached the Wall gap, Kevin could see that Pil and Cort were arguing. Pil was gesturing angrily with his hands, getting into Cort's face, and then Cort shoved Pil in the chest and he fell over. Pil jumped up, hands clenched into fists. 23 stepped between the two boys and grabbed each of their forearms. "Cease your hostilities immediately," it said. Both Pil and Cort tried to pull themselves away from the bot, but 23 tightened its grip.

Suddenly Otter was standing over the bot, holding the hand planer menacingly. "Let go of them now," he said.

"Lower your weapon or I will be forced to aggressively defend myself," said 23.

"Go to hell, you damned bot," said Otter.

Kevin saw that the two adult men had picked up planks of wood and were walking toward the confrontation. 23 let go of Pil, raising its hand toward Otter, and Otter stepped back and triggered the hand planer with a whirr. . . .

Kevin surprised himself by stepping between Otter and 23. "Wait!" he said. He turned to the bot. "23, there's no need to interfere. Pil and Cort fight all the time. It never means anything." 23 hesitated, his arm still raised. Over his shoulder, Kevin could hear the hum of the hand planer and feel Otter's angry tension.

The bot lowered his hand, let go of Cort, and took a step back. "Very well," it said. "Do not overtax your hand today. It is not fully healed." It turned and walked away.

Otter switched the planer off. "Don't ever step into my fight again," he said to Kevin. The two men dropped their planks of wood and turned back to their cabling.

Kevin shrugged, appearing more calm than he felt. "Just saving you from your own funeral," he said. "Maybe you could have taken 23, but I don't think the other bots would've been very happy about it." Otter scowled but spun away without saying anything else.

# CHAPTER 30

THE NEXT MORNING AT SUNRISE THE CAMP CLEARED OUT, LEAVING behind two rebels—one with her left arm in a sling, the other with his foot in a makeshift wooden splint. It was obvious, based on the amount of firepower that the others were packing and their grim, serious demeanors, that something big was about to happen.

"Are they heading to the City?" Nick asked the woman with her arm in a sling. If they were, he needed to be a part of it. He might be able to use the battle chaos to get his parents out. . . .

"No," she said gruffly. "Haven't gotten the orders for that yet."

"So where are they going?" he asked. "What's the plan?"

The woman scowled and said, "If you don't know, then you aren't supposed to know. Now keep quiet, otherwise I'll activate your sister's stun collar just to shut you up."

The other guard limped up on his bad leg. "Don't worry about Jackie," he said to Nick. "She's all rusted out because not only is she missing the action, but now she has to be a babysitter."

"What is the action, exactly?" said Nick.

"Clamp it, Witt," said Jackie, shoving the man on the shoulder, sending him staggering back and forcing him to hop to stay off his bad foot.

"Dammit, Jackie, you trying to break my other foot?" said Witt. Jackie ignored him. Witt hobbled back to Nick. "She's right," he said, giving Nick a slightly apologetic shrug. "You've got a long way to go before getting back in Ro's good graces, now that you've dragged your true-believer sister into our camp."

"Like I told Ro, we had nowhere else to go," Nick said. "And she's not a true believer. She's just . . . she's just confused right now."

"I'm not confused," Cass said. She was sitting on a log near a fire pit, staring into the ashes. She looked up at Nick and Witt. "My parents, my *real* parents, are alive and happy in the City. And that's where my home is."

Witt raised an eyebrow at Nick. "Sounds like a true believer to me," he said.

"You're lucky Ro just gave her a stun collar instead of an execution," Jackie said.

Nick clenched his fists and bit back an angry reply. Farryn shouldered past him and got into Jackie's face. "You're the one who has to figure out whose side you're on," he said. "You happy killing people just like the bots?"

"True believers aren't people," Jackie said, grabbing Farryn's shirt with her good arm. She pushed him back roughly, then pressed a trigger on her comm bracelet. Cass gave a short, choking scream, then fell to the ground, clutching at her neck and kicking her legs spastically.

Lexi ran to Cass, while Nick and Farryn lunged toward Jackie. Witt stepped in front of Jackie, a burst pistol in his hands. "Stop!" he said. Nick and Farryn skidded to a stop. Cass continued to kick and choke in the dirt next to the fire pit, while Lexi knelt next to her, powerless to help. If he moved fast enough, maybe he could disarm Witt before he had a chance to fire . . .

"Jackie, turn off the damned collar!" said Witt.

Jackie reached down to her wrist, slowly, theatrically, and thumbed her bracelet. Cass's legs stopped kicking and she took in a deep sucking breath. She pushed herself up to her knees, retching. Both Farryn and Nick rushed past Witt to Cass. "Are you okay?" said Nick to Cass, holding her shoulder. Farryn stood over them, clenching and unclenching his fists.

Cass stayed on her hands and knees a few more moments,

her ragged breath slowly returning to normal. Then she pushed Nick's hand away and stood. "You brought me here," she said, her voice raspy. "This is your fault."

Nick shook his head but didn't know what to say. He fought back angry tears. She wasn't wrong. He had rescued her, but now here she was, collared and tortured. He turned and walked over to Jackie, who folded her arms over her chest and smirked at him.

"Do that again and I will kill you," he said quietly. "Take her collar off."

Jackie laughed, then shook her head. "That's not gonna happen," she said.

"Take it off," he repeated.

"That's enough," Witt said, grabbing Nick's arm. Nick spun, fist clenched, ready to throw a punch.

Witt stepped back, apparently reading the intent in Nick's eyes, and raised his gun, and Erica, who had been gathering water at the stream, was suddenly there, slipping behind Witt, unsheathing her hunting knife. There was a grinding roar from the south that staggered everyone, followed a moment later by a fireball that rose up over the tree line about a half mile to the south.

"What the . . . ?" said Witt. He pulled an earbud from his pocket and jammed it in his ear, then tapped on his comm bracelet. "Hello? Hello?"

"Don't be an idiot, Witt," said Jackie. "You know they're

on comm lockdown until after the raid tomorrow." She rushed into a nearby tent and came out a few moments later with a burst pistol holstered at her waist. "I'll check it out. Stay here." Jackie ran off into the woods to the south, moving awkwardly because of her arm sling.

Erica looked at Nick and gave a small enigmatic smile, then a nod, and then she took off after Jackie.

"Wait!" said Witt, but he didn't raise his gun, and she quickly disappeared into the trees. Nick could see black smoke rising from the site of the fireball. He took a step toward the woods.

"No," said Witt, raising his weapon. "Stay put."

"If it's a fight, I can help," Nick said. "Let me go. Or shoot me in the back, like a bot would."

Witt hesitated, then nodded and lowered his pistol.

Nick looked at Lexi and Farryn. "Watch my sister," he said.

"Don't be an idiot," said Lexi.

Nick smiled. "It's way too late for that," he said.

Lexi gave him a small smile in return. "Yeah, true," she said.

Nick turned and ran after Jackie and Erica. He headed south at a quick jog, following a game path. His heart was pounding, more from adrenaline and nerves than exertion. The game path ended abruptly and Nick ducked into the trees. His right foot hit a muddy patch of grass and he skidded and almost fell, catching himself on a tree trunk. A blast from nearby to the south rocked him backward, almost knocking him onto the ground. It was followed by a faint scream and then the crackle of burst rifles. Nick hesitated a moment, then ran toward the noise.

Quickly the gunfire grew louder, and Nick slowed to a crouching walk, not wanting to blunder right into the middle of the battle. Ahead, among the trees, he saw smoke and the orange glow of fire and the bright flashes of burst rifles. He dropped to the ground, moving forward on his hands and knees, and then he saw three figures coming toward him out of the smoke and he quickly crawled behind a tree. When the figures grew clearer, he realized it was Erica and a man holding up a third person between them. He was unconscious or dead, his legs dragging uselessly along the ground as Erica and the man struggled to move him away from the fight.

Nick rushed over to the trio. It took him a moment to recognize the third man, because his injuries were so bad. It was Marco. His shirt was soaked with blood and his face and hands had been burned. The skin was raw, red and blistered and peeling, and his eyebrows and most of his hair were gone. "What's happening?" Nick said to Erica, having to yell to be heard over the blast crackles.

"Get out of here!" said the man to Marco's right. They were dragging Marco again, and Nick jogged alongside them. "It's all gone to hell! Stumbled across a group of damned bots, no comm signals, no warnings. Weren't supposed to see any bots for two days!"

Two more men appeared out of the trees, hurrying past them. "Back to camp!" one said as he rushed past.

The man dragging Marco, Nick realized, had two burst rifles slung over his shoulder—one must have been Marco's. "Give me a rifle!" Nick said.

The man unslung one of the rifles and tossed it to Nick without slowing down.

"Keep your head down!" Erica said. "This isn't target practice."

Nick nodded and then ran, crouching, to the south, flicking off the safety of the rifle as he ran and setting the burst to medium. Enough to take down a bot, hopefully, without draining his weapon too quickly.

Nick saw that the smoke in the distance glowed with energy bursts. He recognized the crackling hum of lase blasts. *Peteys.* He couldn't see them through the smoke, but he knew they were nearby. He dropped to the ground. Rifle bursts returned fire from low and to the right, and he saw three rebels tucked down behind two trees, their camo gear blending with the grass and underbrush. He sprinted over in a crouch and dove down next to them. Ro was the man on the far left. "What the hell you doing here?" he said.

"Came to help!" said Nick.

"Get the hell out of here!" Ro growled. "Rendezvous back at the camp!" The air crackled, and a tree limb ten feet to their left exploded and flew backward. Nick flinched instinctively. Ro and the others shot bursts into the smoke, although there were no discernible targets. Another burst came, striking the ground ten feet in front of them, sending dirt flying and making the ground shudder. Nick sighted down the scope of Marco's rifle. At first he saw only smoke and vague darting shadows. Then he felt something shift in his robotic eye and he almost reflexively took a hand off his gun to touch his face. It didn't hurt, exactly, but it felt odd, like something crawling over his eyeball, and then the smoke was somehow transparent. He still knew it was there, but he could see through it clearly, even though that shouldn't have been possible.

In the distance, barely visible, he saw the darting spherical shape of a scout hovering among the trees. It vanished behind tree cover, and he waited. When it reappeared, he tracked it, squeezed the trigger, and watched as an instant later it erupted into flaming shrapnel.

"Yes!" he yelled.

"What the hell?" said Ro. Nick didn't answer. A Petey had appeared from behind tree cover off in the distance, near where the wrecked sphere bot lay. It raised its lase arm toward their position, and Nick sighted quickly and fired, and the burst hit the Petey square in its chest. It staggered back into a tree, then raised itself back up.

"Damn!" said Nick. "Medium burst won't take the Peteys down?"

"Need a full burst to even slow them down much," said Ro. "But you can't get a good shot in this smoke."

"I can see fine," Nick said. He squeezed off another round, tagging the Petey again, disrupting its aim as it was firing. The bot's lase burst shot harmlessly into the air. Nick sighted another scout bot and squeezed off a burst, but the bot was weaving in and out of the trees and the shot missed. He focused on the bot, watching its flight, sensing its pattern, and he tracked in front of it, leading it, and somehow the bot's frantic bob and weave seemed to slow way down, like it was flying through honey, and Nick released a burst that struck the bot squarely and destroyed it. *Two*, Nick thought, his fingers tingling with adrenaline. *That's two bots down.*

There was a blur of movement to his left and then Erica was sliding down beside him, her pistol in her hand, the right side of her body pressing against his leg and arm. "Still alive?" she said.

He flashed her a quick grin. "So far," he said.

Ro triggered his comm bracelet. "Anybody else still pinned down?" he said. "Report positions." Ro listened for a few moments, his hand over his ear to shield his earpiece from the noise. "Okay," he said, clapping Nick on the shoulder. "Everyone alive is getting out. Let's go."

Ro stood, preparing to run, and then Nick saw another Petey, at the edge of his range, aim its lase arm. "Down!" he said, slamming his shoulder against Ro and knocking him over. The Petey's lase burst crackled overhead, through the spot where Ro had been standing. Nick took aim at the Petey and triggered three quick medium bursts, knocking the bot backward into the trees. Erica fired her pistol, four rapid shots, but her bursts were wild. She obviously couldn't see through the smoke like Nick.

"Okay, it's down!" said Nick.

"Come on!" said Ro. He grabbed the back of Nick's shirt and hauled him to his feet. Nick had a wild impulse to ignore Ro, to run toward the bots to get better aim, to switch to full burst and see if he could take down one of the big Peteys, but then he thought of his sister, collared, needing him even though she hated him, and his brother, lost God knew where. He slung the rifle over his shoulder and followed Erica and the retreating rebels.

# CHAPTER 31

THE REBELS SCRAMBLED BACK INTO CAMP IN GROUPS OF TWO AND THREE, many nursing wounds—everything from minor burns and cuts to one man who Cass couldn't believe was still alive. He was unconscious, but she could see his chest rising and falling with his ragged breaths as he was carried past her by two unhurt rebels. His right arm was gone halfway up the bicep, a blackened charred stump. It looked as if the lase blast had cauterized the wound, which at least had kept him from bleeding to death.

Nick jogged into view, a rifle slung over his shoulder. He seemed unhurt, and Cass felt a huge surge of relief that caught her by surprise. How much had she actually been worrying about him, this boy who had stolen her from the City? Lexi brushed past Cass, running over to Nick and giving him a kiss and a long hug.

"Wounded to med tent now!" bellowed Ro, striding into camp. "Everyone who can stand, break down the camp! We leave in one hour and we're not coming back!"

Ro grabbed the medic's arm as she rushed past him, and she spun to a halt. "Get the wounded walking," he said to her. "We can't stay here."

She shrugged out of his grip. "I'll do what I can," she said. "But there are gonna be a few who won't be able to leave."

Ro shook his head. He took a deep breath, held it a few moments, then said, "Report to me in an hour. We'll see where we stand then." The medic nodded and ran off.

Ro walked up to Cass. As he drew closer, she could see that a line of blood had dried in a trail down the side of his face. Behind him, Cass saw Nick break away from Lexi's hug and turn to watch Ro intently. Ro reached for his comm bracelet. Cass tensed but didn't say a word. He could stun her if he wanted to, but she wouldn't give him the satisfaction of crying out. She'd bite off her tongue first, if she had to. He thumbed his bracelet and Cass flinched, despite her best effort, her body expecting the shock that didn't come. She cursed herself silently for the weakness.

Ro held his hand out. "Your collar will come off now," he said. "Snap it apart in the back."

Nick was smiling behind him, but she didn't smile

back—he might interpret that as gratitude, which she definitely didn't want him to think she felt. She reached behind her neck and pulled the collar apart with a *click*. She ignored Ro's waiting hand and tossed it onto the ground at his feet, glaring at him, then massaged the skin on her throat where the collar had been chafing. "Why?" she said.

He bent and picked up the collar, snapping it shut in his hand. "It's a favor to your brother." He pointed the collar at Cass. "But I still don't trust you, and this can go right back onto your neck if it needs to."

Cass crossed her arms over her chest and held his stare. He stared back, waiting for her to flinch. Then he actually gave her a small smile and an almost imperceptible nod. He turned to Nick. "She's your responsibility."

Nick nodded. "Understood," he said.

Ro frowned. "Not that she could do much damage right now anyway," he said. "The bots seem to know where we are." He walked quickly away, barking orders as he headed toward his tent.

"If you're expecting a thank-you, it's going to be a long wait," Cass said to Nick.

Nick smiled. "That almost sounds like the old Cass," he said.

Cass didn't know how to respond, so she just turned away.

"We need to be ready to hike," Nick said. "Ro's right, the bots are too close." He turned to Lexi and Farryn, and Erica, who Cass hadn't even seen arrive. "I still think it's best to stick with the rebels," he said quietly, just loud enough for their small group to hear. "They'll be our best shot at getting news about Kevin. And when they attack the City, I want to be part of it."

Lexi and Farryn nodded, and Erica shrugged but didn't object. Cass sat down in the dirt. That City that Nick was so eager to attack contained her birth parents. And her little sister. Why should she cooperate? Why in the world should she let herself be dragged around the woods?

"What are you doing?" said Nick.

"I'm not going with you," Cass said.

"Cass, there's no time for this," said Nick.

"You better go get that collar back from Ro, then," Cass said. "There's no other way you're going to get me to walk out with you."

"Dammit, Cass!" said Nick. "I'm your brother! The bots are the enemy!"

"It's not that simple," Cass said.

"Cass, we've got to go!" Nick said.

Cass just shook her head.

Lexi stepped between Nick and Cass and squatted down, putting her forearms on her thighs. "Cass," she said quietly, "I know you're confused, but be reasonable. The bots aren't going to take you back. They'll kill you."

Cass shook her head again, refusing to even consider what

Lexi was saying. "You're not going to have any more luck than my brother, Lexi," she said.

Lexi stood, throwing her hands up in frustration. Farryn walked over to his pack and opened a flap, digging inside. He pulled Cass's self-portrait and a pen out of his pack and walked over to Cass. She frowned at him. Did he really think he was going to make a difference? "You've already shown me this," she said.

He knelt down and held the paper out to Cass, blank side up. "Draw something," he said.

Cass stared at Farryn, her heart suddenly racing. "That's stupid," she whispered.

"Draw," Farryn said.

"What would I draw?" Cass said.

"How about your brother Kevin," he said.

Cass shook her head. "I don't know what he looks like," she said.

"Then just draw a boy. Any boy," said Farryn. He nudged her gently with the pen. "Come on."

Cass slowly reached out and took the paper and pen. She set the paper on a nearby flat rock and tentatively began to draw. Her hand moved slowly, and it was such an effort to form the oval of a face, to keep her hand from shaking the pen right out of her grip. But slowly her grip steadied, and her lines grew more confident, and her hand began to move more quickly, almost as if by magic, and it became like she was watching her hand draw and had no control over it. The pen flew over the page, and a face emerged. After a minute she was done, and she dropped the pen and stared. She knew the face staring back at her from the paper. It was her little brother, Kevin. She knew him. Her temples suddenly pounded and she had to squint and put her hand on the ground to keep her balance, and then her stomach twisted, and a wave of nausea overcame her, and she vomited in the dirt.

# CHAPTER 32

KEVIN'S BURNS HEALED IN TWO DAYS. WITH HIS HAND BACK, IT WAS time to try to escape again. But he wasn't sure how. The Wall gap climb wouldn't work again—maybe he should just find a quiet, dark spot and climb the Wall? No, the perimeter alarms were probably active for the whole Wall.

He lay in bed and considered the problem, staring unfocused at the ceiling. He'd have to find some way to disable the alarm, or at least trick it into ignoring him. He couldn't get caught again—he had to assume that 23 and Dr. Winston weren't bluffing about a second failed escape being treated harshly. If Captain Clay got involved—he felt a nervous tingling in his hands at the thought. Whatever punishment she came up with, it would be brutal.

So how to beat the perimeter sensor? He tapped his fingers one by one on his forehead as he brainstormed. Maybe it was a matter of thinking of the alarm like a circuit—he just had to find a way to keep the circuit unbroken, to bridge the gap that his body was creating. So that led to the next question—what type of sensor was being used? Electromagnetic? Optical? Something else?

"Rise and shine!" said Otter, lifting the side of Kevin's mattress and dumping him onto the floor.

Kevin landed hard on his elbows and knees, bruising himself on the hard floor. "Rust!" he said. He pushed himself up and glared at Otter, who ignored him, whistling and walking to the showers.

At breakfast, Otter sat with Wex at a separate table from the other boys and girls. Was this the Island equivalent of dating? Kevin wondered. Kevin almost laughed out loud— Otter was somehow managing to keep his biceps flexed the entire meal. It must have been exhausting, actually, Kevin thought. It looked like he was trying to arm wrestle his fork.

After their meal, 23 was waiting for Kevin outside the mess hall. "The Governor has requested to see you in his laboratory," it said.

"Let me check my schedule," said Kevin. Pil laughed. Even Cort smiled briefly. 23 ignored the remark and began walking. Kevin followed.

"Why's the Governor so interested in me?" Kevin asked.

"I do not know, and I will not speculate," said 23.

"Yeah," said Kevin. "Thanks for the help."

They continued on in silence. 23 led him back to the Governor's lab in his cellar and opened the door. "Enter," it said. "I will wait outside."

Dr. Winston was waiting for Kevin in the lab, leaning back against the worktable he had used to operate on bot 6. He wore his stained work smock and had a set of scope glasses pushed up at his forehead.

"How is your hand?" Dr. Winston asked when Kevin came down the stairs.

"Fine," Kevin said cautiously.

"Clever idea, the modified solder," said Dr. Winston. "But poor execution."

"Well, I didn't have much time to work on it," said Kevin.

"Yes, I suppose so," said Dr. Winston. He straightened and walked over to the metal cabinet on the wall that Kevin had noticed last time he was in the lab. "Come," he said. "I want to show you something."

"Why?" said Kevin, not moving. "What's going on? Why do you care about my hand? Why do you want to show me stuff?"

"Kevin," said Dr. Winston, "now that your hand is healed, do you plan on trying to escape again?"

Kevin knew it would be useless to lie, so he said nothing.

"Yes, of course you do," Dr. Winston said, shaking his head.

He sighed. "Kevin, I had a strange feeling about you when you were brought in. Déjà vu, almost. Do you know what that is?"

Kevin shook his head no.

"I felt as though I had seen you before. Like I already knew you. Have we met, Kevin?"

"No," Kevin said.

"No, we haven't," Dr. Winston said. He moved back to the worktable and laid his hands on its surface, leaning forward. "I ran a genetic assay from samples gathered without your knowledge—hair, skin cells, et cetera. I was following a hunch." He paused. "The results were very interesting."

Kevin could feel his heart pounding in his ears. What was Dr. Winston hinting at?

Dr. Winston reached down to a shelf under the work table and picked up a small vid screen. He tapped it a few times, stared at it with a sad smile, and then held it up for Kevin to see. "Kevin, do you recognize this man?"

Kevin stared at the 3D image of a man in his twenties with a head of thick brown hair and a skinny, pale face. It took him a moment, and then it hit him almost like a physical blow. "That's my father," Kevin said. "My father, when he was . . . younger. How'd you get that?"

"I took it," said Dr. Winston. "Thirty years ago. It's a photo of my son."

# CHAPTER 33

THE REBEL WHO HAD LOST AN ARM DIED—HEART ATTACK INDUCED BY shock, Nick overheard the medic say. One other rebel, a woman, had died on the battlefield. Everyone else was able to break camp and hike out.

Thankfully, after drawing the picture of Kevin, Cass seemed willing to travel with them. It was a breakthrough, he knew, a sign that a few of her memories were starting to come back. But Nick was worried about her—it was apparently physically traumatic, the jumbled fight that her mind was going through. She seemed weak and dizzy and had thrown up twice more. He was making sure she kept sipping water, so that she didn't dehydrate, but there was little else he could do to help.

Also, he had to admit, he was a little annoyed that Farryn had been able to reach her, when he, her own brother, had failed.

Because of the wounded and the amount of gear they were carrying, the group of seventy or so stretched over a quarter mile and moved slowly. Nobody was complaining, though—not the wounded who limped along painfully, nor the men and women burdened with double loads in order to lighten the packs of the wounded. Everyone seemed to silently agree that they had no choice. The bots had been a mere half mile from the camp. The site was no longer safe. They had to move, or wait for the bots to come back and finish the job.

They headed northwest. Nick assumed they were moving to another hidden campsite, but his attempts to ask the rebels where they were heading, and how far they had to go, were met with silence or even outright hostility. So much for whatever goodwill he had gained from the battle, Nick thought.

They walked all day, mostly in silence. Nick tried to speak to Cass, but she didn't respond. She did nod, and accept drinks from his canteen when he offered, which was something, at least.

As the day was fading into evening, she surprised him by saying, out of the blue, "I remember a big campfire, and lots of kids. Did I . . . did we do that a lot?" Her arms were folded across her chest, like she was angry or cold, and she wouldn't look Nick in the eye.

Nick took a moment to calm the rush of excitement he felt. "Yes," he said. "Kidbons. Bonfires for the kids at the Freepost, whenever the Council had its weekly meeting." He tried hard to sound neutral. His instincts told him that if he seemed too excited, too eager, he would scare her off.

Cass nodded. "Kidbons. Yes. Kidbons." She drifted back toward where Farryn was walking. Nick could see Erica farther behind—she had offered to take a rear guard.

"She's remembering," Nick said quietly to Lexi. "She's coming back."

Lexi took his hand and gave it a squeeze. "It's good," she said. "Really good. But it still might take a while. You can't rush her."

Nick nodded. Lexi held on to his hand and pulled him closer. Nick's heart sped up. Was she about to kiss him?

"Nick," she said, whispering, "the rebels are never going to trust Cass."

Nick frowned. "When her memory comes back fully, it'll be fine. . . ."

"What about the way we found her? Just waiting for us on the road? Ro's letting that go for now, but he won't forget."

It was odd, Nick agreed. Very strange. But what could he do?

"We should leave the rebels," Lexi said. "You, me, Farryn, and Cass."

Nick shook his head. "And Erica? What about her?"

"We don't owe anything to Erica!" Lexi whispered angrily. "I still think she'll lase us in the back someday."

Nick felt a rush of annoyance. *This again!* "Look, Lexi, just because you're jealous doesn't mean you can call Erica a traitor."

"Jealous!" Lexi said loudly. "You . . ." she said, her voice again an angry whisper, "you are a moron." She strode away.

"Lexi, wait!" Nick said, but he let her go. He knew that anything else he said would probably just make it worse.

That evening they set up a makeshift camp near a dry creek bed spotted with low boulders. As night fell Ro called the entire group together, except for three of the worst wounded who were already resting among the rocks, and four perimeter scout guards, who were spread out twenty-five yards beyond the camp in each of the cardinal directions.

"I'll keep this quick," Ro said, just loudly enough for everyone to hear. "We lost Cooper and Michaela today to the bots. They were good fighters, and loyal friends, and they will be missed. The bots have the blood of two more on their hands." He hesitated. "I risked brief comm contact with the three other rendezvous squads, and none of them have been attacked. We were the only lucky ones. Regardless, the mission has been aborted. We don't know if it was a breach in our comm security or just bad luck that put those bots in our path, but the other squad leaders and I agree that we've already been too compromised to continue with the attack right now."

A few of the rebels grumbled angrily. Next to Nick, one man spoke up. "So we just give up that quickly?"

Ro took a step toward the man. He said nothing for a few moments, collecting himself, and then said, his voice low but tight, "We're a day's hike from our northwest campsite, maybe a day and a half with our wounded. We go there, we heal up, and then we plan a way to kill some bots. A lot of bots. Got it?" The man nodded, and Ro held eye contact, then nodded back. Ro raised his voice again to readdress the group. "Okay, everyone have their guard shifts for the night?" The men and women nodded. "Then get to it," Ro said.

That night Nick lay on the sandy ground of the creek bed near his sister. She didn't say anything, but she didn't get up and move, at least. He was hoping that Lexi would lie down nearby, but she pointedly found a spot on the other side of the creek bed, behind a boulder that blocked her from his view. Nick sighed. *Well, one problem at a time*, he thought.

"Cass," Nick said, then waited.

Cass was silent, and Nick felt a pang of disappointment, but then she rolled over and said, "Yes?"

"Cass, I'm sorry for this. For the way you've been treated. For all you've been through."

She didn't reply.

Nick looked up at the night sky between the trees. It was a bright night, the moon nearly full, with only a few clouds. A light breeze rustled the leaves gently.

"You were dying, Cass," Nick said. "The bots had shot you, and you fell on a branch and it went right through your lung. You were bleeding to death." Nick saw his sister again lying there in a puddle of blood, her face ghostly white, the stick jutting from her chest. He blinked hard, breathed deeply to dispel the image. "Letting the bots take you was my only option. I couldn't let you die. Cass, do you remember any of it?"

Nick waited but was met with only silence. He sighed and closed his eyes.

"A bit," Cass said, so softly that Nick could barely hear. He opened his eyes. "I remember the pain," Cass said, "and lying in a puddle . . . and I'm starting . . . I'm starting to remember things about you, and the Freepost."

"That's good," Nick said, blinking hard to fight back the sudden sting in his eyes. "That's really good."

Cass sat up and looked at Nick. He sat up too. "But listen, Nick," she said. "My family in the City—those really are my birth parents, and that is my sister."

"Okay, Cass," said Nick. "I believe you." He wasn't sure if he did, but it was possible, and Cass certainly believed it. There was no point in arguing with her now, not with things moving in the right direction.

Cass lay back down. "They're not the enemy," she said. "They're family . . . like you."

"Okay, Cass," Nick said. "Get some sleep."

Nick watched the sky and the swaying leaves in the moonlight until he heard his sister's breathing deepen and slow, and then he shut his eyes, feeling the most hopeful that he had let himself feel in a while. His sister was coming back to him. She had called him family. Kevin would be next. He'd be in a group of refugees, or they'd find someone who knew where he was, or they'd walk into a Freepost and he'd be waiting there, probably tinkering with the grid. . . . Nick had to believe it. He had to. Slowly, he drifted to sleep.

"Bots!" Nick was woken by Erica yelling, seemingly in his ear. "Bots from the south, half mile, closing fast!"

Nick felt a moment of fuzzy confusion—was he dreaming? But then he woke fully. He scrambled to his feet as the other rebels did the same. He grabbed the burst rifle that Ro had let him keep. Then he froze. What to do about Cass? And Lexi? Lexi and Farryn came running up with pistols in their hands. They were both terrible shots, and could barely hit a tree from ten yards away, Nick knew, but still, better to be armed than completely defenseless. "Stay with Cass!" he said. Farryn nodded.

Nick turned to run south, but Lexi grabbed his shirt. "Stay alive!" she said. "I'm not done being mad at you!" She tugged him toward her and pressed a quick, hard kiss onto his lips, then pushed him away.

He grinned—and then he turned and ran into the trees to the south.

Soon he slowed to a fast walk. Even with the strong moon-light, it wasn't bright enough to be running full speed through the trees; he'd break his neck. He also didn't know what he was heading into.

There was an explosion of light and sound to his left. A tree shattered into flame and Nick flung himself to the ground. To his left and right he could see, now in flickering firelight, that other rebels crouched low. Nick didn't have a comm bracelet, so he wasn't patched into their communication—there was no way for him to know if there was any plan, any organization, any sense yet of what they were up against. He peered into the trees to the south, looking for the bot that had lased the tree, but saw nothing. He tried sighting through the scope of his rifle, but he could only make out the outlines of trees in the murky light, and then something in his robot eye adjusted with an audible whirr, leaving him dizzy and queasy for a moment.

The forest, through his bot eye, was brightly lit with a bluish tint. There—yes, he could see two scout spheres, and behind them, a soldier bot. He thumbed his rifle to medium burst, took aim, and quickly squeezed off two shots, taking down the spheres. The night was lit by their flaming shells, exposing the soldier bot, which ducked behind tree cover as nearby rebels opened fire.

Two bursts from the rebels hit the tree sheltering the bot, shattering the trunk, and the bot rushed forward, lases blast-ing from both arms. One shot burst short and to the right of

Nick, plowing a shower of dirt into the air; another blast connected a mere fifteen feet to his left. Nick felt the heat, and there was a brief scream and a rebel stood, bathed in flames. His clothes, his hair, his face—the flames were eating him like a log in a bonfire. He staggered forward ten feet, arms out wide, mouth open in a silent scream, and then fell forward onto his face. The flames continued to flicker on the body, and the smell hit Nick. It was a combination of smoke, burned hair, and—this made Nick fight not to retch—charred meat.

The rebels nearby returned the bot's fire, and a few shots hit their mark, staggering but not stopping the soldier bot. Nick forced the thought of the burned man out of his mind and focused on the bot. It was moving quickly, but Nick's bot eye had no trouble tracking it. He flicked his rifle to autoburst and held down the trigger, releasing five shots in rapid succession. The first shot hit the bot in the arm and didn't even slow it; the second and third hit the bot's legs, staggering it; the fourth and fifth hit the bot square in the chest, knocking it down. As it struggled to rise it became an easy target, and a flurry of rebel fire slammed it from four or five different guns. The bot almost rose, despite the barrage, and then fell back to the ground. The onslaught continued on the now defenseless bot, and after a few more moments of rifle bursts detonating, its armor cracked and the bot exploded with a roar and a scattering rain of neo-plas and metal.

The air nearby filled with lase blasts again as three more

soldier bots appeared behind the remains of the destroyed bot. Nick frantically began firing, but the bots were moving fast, and their lases were flying past and bursting against nearby trees and hitting the ground. With the deafening noise and the shaking ground, it was almost impossible to get off steady, well-aimed shots, especially since he was expecting every lase blast from the bots to hit him and turn him into a charred corpse. He forced down the panic, the instinct to run. He steadied his breathing and concentrated on his aim. Almost every one of his shots found its mark, but many of the other rebels' shots were wild, and the bots were still advancing. As the bots drew closer, though, they presented better targets, and more rifle bursts began landing directly on the bots' armor. The bots slowed, and Nick began to let himself think that maybe, just maybe, they'd be able to take these bots down, too, and then a soldier bot appeared from the trees twenty feet to Nick's right.

The world seemed to slow down, and Nick felt strangely calm. He knew he was about to die. The bots had distracted the rebels and flanked them while they weren't paying attention. A rifle burst blasted the bot's armored back, then another, and Nick saw Ro standing behind the bot, firing, but the robot didn't even seem to notice. Nick rolled over and raised his rifle, but he knew it wouldn't be in time, because the bot already had both lase arms aimed at him.

A red light flared from the bot's chest and lit on Nick's face, momentarily blinding him, and then the bot turned away.

Without firing.

Nick was still alive.

The bot aimed its lases at Ro. Blasts from the other three bots still erupted among the rebels, pinning them down, so nobody else was able to lend aid. Nick thumbed his rifle to full burst—his battery pack would be depleted for at least a minute after the shot, he knew—and released the burst into the back of the bot's neck just as Ro, screaming angrily, released a full burst directly into the bot's face. The combined bursts snapped the bot's neck. It staggered, its head hanging sideways against its left shoulder, then froze and fell like a statue to the ground.

Nick crawled behind the bot, putting its armored body between himself and the three remaining bots. Ro had the same idea, and joined him behind the dead bot. "You're a lucky bastard," said Ro.

"You too," said Nick.

"The bot had you and didn't take the shot."

Nick just shrugged. He didn't know what had happened, why he was still alive. Ro didn't say anything else, and they waited, the battle raging around them, while their depleted rifles recharged.

No more bots appeared, and within fifteen minutes, the three remaining bots were overcome by rebel fire thanks in large part to Nick's deadly accurate marksmanship. Two more rebels were killed in the effort, though—a lase blast in the chest when the man ran for better cover, and a woman with terrible luck who was crushed by a falling tree that had been felled by friendly fire.

Nick and the others returned to the camp. Nick's adrenaline was just starting to fade—he was forming a terrible headache and was incredibly thirsty—and he kept seeing the image of the charred man, staggering forward and then smoldering in the dirt. Still, he also felt a current of excitement. He had survived. He had killed bots. More than that—without his help, the rebels probably would have all been killed.

Back at the dry creek bed, Nick's stomach lurched when he saw a broken scout bot lying among the rocks. The bots had made it to the camp? "Cass!" he called out. "Lexi! Farryn!" There was no answer.

# CHAPTER 34

CASS CROUCHED BEHIND A ROCK IN THE DRY CREEK BED, FARRYN AND Lexi next to her, nervously clutching their small weapons. Rebels ran past. She could hear the crackle of lase fire and rifle bursts and, occasionally, screams.

She looked at Farryn and Lexi. They weren't paying attention to her; they were focused outward, huddling against the rock for cover. It would be so easy to slip away. She'd be up and running before they had a chance to react, and in the chaos of the battle they'd never find her. She could make her way back to the City, and her birth parents, and her sister. . . .

But no. She stayed put. She was beginning to remember; every day, every hour, it seemed, more details of who she used to be trickled into her mind, but everything was still hazy. The

City wasn't home anymore. She couldn't go back, even if they would take her. But she still didn't feel at home in the forest, either, or like she belonged with Nick and Kevin. Certainly she didn't belong with the rebels, who had collared her. She was in limbo, not quite belonging anywhere, with anybody.

She ducked as a lase blast crackled nearby. *For now,* she told herself, *just stay alive. Figure out your other problems later.* There was another loud burst of lase fire, followed by rifle bursts and shouting, and then a sphere bot suddenly appeared from among the trees. It headed toward them.

Cass stood to run but then saw a whir of movement to her right and Farryn yelled, "Look out!" and crashed into her, knocking her back to the ground. Her ears filled with a deafening buzzing crackle and she could hear Lexi yelling and firing her pistol. She was blinded by a flash of light, and a burst of heat washed over her body. On top of her, Farryn screamed, painfully loud right by her ear, and she felt his whole body go stiff, then limp.

"Farryn!" Cass yelled, her voice muffled with her face pressed against the ground. He didn't move. She struggled frantically to push out from underneath him. Just as she was getting up, another explosion knocked her back down. She was dazed for a moment, and then a strong hand was lifting her up.

The first thing that registered was the sphere bot, broken and smoking on the ground nearby. Then a woman's face loomed in front of her. She was a rebel, with short blond hair. "You okay?" the woman said.

Cass hesitated, looking down at herself. Was she hurt? No . . . she seemed okay. She nodded. "Fine," she said.

The woman pointed at Farryn. "Get your friend to the medic as soon as you can." She turned away and ran into the woods.

Cass looked at Farryn. He lay facedown in the dirt. He wasn't moving. His pants were scorched, the canvas completely burned off the right leg, the shoe and sock somehow missing, revealing a wound that made Cass suck in her breath. The calf was jaggedly cut, and burned. The burn had stopped the bleeding, but the skin was blistered and raw and peeling away, and the cut ran to the bone. Cass felt a rush of nausea that she ignored. Lexi bent over Farryn and felt his neck.

"He's alive," she said, looking up at Cass.

"What happened?" Cass said.

"Bot was coming right at us and Farryn shielded you, and then the rebel and I took it down."

Farryn had indeed shielded her, Cass realized. He had saved her life. And he may be dying because of it. She wanted to cry, but now was not the time. "Come on," she said. "We need to get him help."

Cass and Lexi struggled to drape Farryn's arms over their shoulders, then managed to stand, Farryn hanging limply between them. They began hauling him slowly toward where they hoped the medic was. His wounded leg dragged in the dirt, which made Cass wince to think about, but it couldn't be helped.

Farryn groaned and began to feebly struggle. "Where?" he said. "What?"

"You're hurt," Cass said. "We're getting you to the medic."

"Hurts," Farryn said. "Leg hurts so bad."

"I know," said Cass. "The medic will help. Can you lift the injured leg off the ground? Can you lean on us and hop on the other leg?"

Farryn managed to lift his bad leg and put some weight on his good leg. He was still leaning heavily on the girls, but they were no longer dragging deadweight and began to move faster. He even offered Cass a weak smile, which Cass thought was one of the bravest things she had ever seen.

Cass was still fighting back tears. Was she going to lose Farryn, this boy she was just starting to remember? Just when she was getting something back, something that felt important somehow, was it going to be snatched away from her, just like her sister and parents had been?

They made it to the bank of the creek bed and thankfully saw the medic twenty yards away, where she had set her bedroll for the night. She was busy bandaging a man's arm wound. A woman lay on the ground nearby, her shirt bloody. The woman wasn't breathing, and her mouth hung open.

The medic had finished the bandaging by the time Cass

and Lexi managed to get Farryn over to her. She pointed to the ground at her feet. "Set him down," she said.

"Help her first," Farryn said, nodding weakly at the woman who lay on the ground.

"She's gone," the medic said. "Beyond any help but God's." She helped Lexi and Cass ease Farryn to the ground, then knelt down to examine his leg. "If there is a God, that is," she muttered. She took a pair of scissors from her belt pack and cut away the remaining scraps of Farryn's pant leg. She was careful, but even her slight jostling made Farryn groan with pain.

"Sorry," he said. "Hurts."

"Course it does," the medic said. "It's a damned mess."

Cass knelt next to Farryn's head and laid a hand on his shoulder. She put her other hand on his forehead and brushed his hair back from his eyes. "Can you give him something for the pain?" she said to the medic.

The medic shook her head. "We're in the woods, not a hospital," she said. "I've got very little."

"It's okay," Farryn whispered. He put his hand over Cass's and held it on his shoulder. "Just stay here, okay?"

Cass nodded, not trusting herself to speak.

"Third-degree burns, deep-tissue laceration," the medic said quietly to herself. "Heat cauterized the bleeding but caused extensive muscle damage." She stood up, sighing. "I've got a bit of antibiotic I can spare. We'll keep it clean and hopefully stave off infection until we can get to a Freepost, where I can do more."

Cass stood and whispered, "Is he going to be okay?"

The medic stepped away from Farryn and dug through her pack, pulling out an injector. She hesitated, then pulled out a second injector. "If he stays out of shock, and survives the night, and avoids infection, he'll pull through." She bent down and injected Farryn on the hip with the first shot. "Antibiotic," she said. Then she gave him the second injection. Within a few moments of the second shot, Farryn's body relaxed, his breathing slowed, and he slumped back, closing his eyes. "Painkiller and sedative. Won't last the night, but at least he'll have a few quiet hours." She squatted and took another look at his leg, then stood. "The leg's gotta go," she said. "No way to avoid that, unless you've got a rejuve tank you're hiding somewhere. I'd just like to get him to a Freepost first, so I don't have to amputate out here in the woods."

# CHAPTER 35

KEVIN LAY ON HIS BUNK. HE AND THE OTHER BOYS HAD THE MORNING off work—a rare break. He thought he might sleep in, but he had too many thoughts churning through his mind. The Governor was Dr. Winston. Dr. Winston was his grandfather. The man who had basically created the bots. Kevin didn't know what to make of it. He didn't know what to do next.

His grandfather seemed content hiding in the woods tinkering with his bots, but Kevin didn't have time to just sit around the Island and wait for him to change his mind. Kevin's brother and sister were out in the woods somewhere, looking for him. And his parents were still stuck in the City, his mother still—hurt. Kevin felt a wave of sadness. Did his mother remember him yet? He had to leave, whether or not his grandfather wanted him to.

It would be a whole lot easier if he could convince his grandfather to open the gates and let him walk out, though, since he still hadn't figured out how to disarm or bypass the perimeter alarm.

Otter interrupted Kevin's thoughts with his usual wake-up, dumping Kevin out of bed. "Up," he said. "The girls are waiting for us at the mess hall. Wex said Becca likes your face, for some reason, so you gotta be there."

Kevin pushed himself to his feet. He didn't even know which one Becca was; he had only seen the girls a few times and had barely spoken to any of them. He didn't like the sound of this.

He tried to think of something to say to Otter that would get him out of the breakfast. Maybe that he wasn't feeling well? Otter would just laugh or punch him. Or both, most likely.

The ground shook and he heard a muffled boom in the distance. "What the hell was that?" he said.

Otter, Pil, and Cort were already throwing on clothes. Kevin quickly put on a shirt and pants, stepped into his boots without lacing them, and followed the others out the door.

Smoke was rising from the direction of the mess hall. Islanders were running toward the smoke. Otter took off at a dead sprint, and Kevin and the others followed.

Kevin followed the path around a corner and skidded

to a halt. The mess hall was gone. In its place was burning wreckage.

A crowd was starting to gather, including a handful of bots, one of which Kevin recognized as 23. What had happened? A bomb? Among the crowd were the orphan girls, all except Wex. One girl was screaming and pointing at the remains of the mess hall. "Wex was inside! The bots blew it up!"

Otter rushed toward the wreckage, but 23 stepped forward and grabbed him as he ran past, roughly stopping him in his tracks. "It is not safe," said 23.

"Wex is in there!" Otter said, grabbing 23's arm. "Let me go!"

"There has been an accident," said 23. "It is not safe to enter right now."

"It wasn't an accident!" said the girl. "Two bots were working on the mess hall gridlines and then they started running and then it exploded!"

"I repeat," said 23, "there has been an accident, a malfunction of the power grid—"

Otter struggled against the bot, which continued to hold him tight. "I said let me go, you damned bot!" said Otter. His face was bright red, a mask of exertion and rage. He balled his right hand into a fist and slammed it into a leather patch on 23's cheek. 23 staggered back a step, its head whiplashing, but it didn't release Otter. There was a crackle of energy, a brief flare of light from 23's hand, and Otter fell to the ground, convulsing.

"I regret having to take coercive measures to restrain you," said 23.

There was a communal growl of outrage from the gathered crowd, which pressed forward, and the five bots gathered closer to each other, facing the people. "The remaining Island robots will be arriving shortly," began 23, and then someone threw a rock that hit 23 in the face, and that was the trigger that released the Islanders' anger.

The crowd rushed the bots, and the air crackled with energy from stun blasts. Men and women went down, but there were too many Islanders for the bots to stop, and they were overpowered, disappearing under a tangle of flailing, screaming, growling people.

Kevin saw 23 taken down by four men. They were kicking it and one was pounding a rock, repeatedly, on 23's flattened face. "Stop!" Kevin screamed. He tried to push his way through the crowd, but he was knocked down in the chaos, someone's elbow landing hard on his forehead.

Kevin tried to stand, but he kept getting jostled. Through the crowd he saw 23's arms reach up and twitch spastically, then flop lifelessly to the ground, while the Islander continued to pound its face with the rock. "Stop!" Kevin cried again, finally pushing through the crowd and approaching where 23 lay on the ground. Its arms gave one last twitch, and then the bot stopped moving completely. Kevin felt sick as he took in the bot's flattened face. It was over.

# CHAPTER 36

NICK RAN FRANTICALLY THROUGH THE CAMPSITE, CALLING OUT HIS sister's name, and Lexi's, and Farryn's. Finally he heard Lexi say, "Over here!" and he rushed over to the medic, dizzy with relief.

His relief vanished when he saw Farryn. Farryn was lying on the ground, asleep or unconscious, his head in Cass's lap. He looked pale, and his breathing was shallow, and his right leg was bandaged from the knee down.

Lexi stood and hugged him tightly. Cass remained on the ground with Farryn, but she did give him a brief, weak smile.

"What happened?" he said. "How bad is he hurt?"

"A sphere bot," said Lexi. "I shot it, and one of the rebels shot it, too, and it exploded on Farryn."

"He shielded me from the explosion," said Cass. "The medic said he's going to lose his leg."

"Rust," whispered Nick.

"What about you?" said Lexi. "What happened? How many bots were there?"

"Five or six," said Nick. "We took them down." He no longer had any desire to rehash the battle.

Nick wanted to hear more about Farryn's injury, but Ro strode up and grabbed Nick roughly on the shoulder. "Come with me," he said. He nodded at Cass and Lexi. "You two also."

"What's going on?" said Nick.

Ro started walking without answering. Nick and Lexi followed, and after Cass carefully extracted herself from Farryn, she joined them. Ro led them back to the creek bed, where a group of ten rebels, and Erica, was waiting. Two men were holding Erica by her forearms. Her jaw was set hard—she looked so angry that Nick wouldn't have been surprised if she tried to take on all the rebels herself. All their packs—Erica's, Lexi's, Farryn's, Cass's, and Nick's— lay piled in a heap, opened, their few belongings scattered in the dirt.

"Scan them," said Ro. "Thoroughly. Slowly. Don't miss an inch. Nick first."

"I've already been scanned," said Nick. One of the rebels stepped forward with the scanner. He bent down and began very slowly moving the scanner up Nick's left leg. "You don't trust me?" said Nick. "Without me, the bots would have killed all of you today!"

"Or maybe without you, the bots would never have found us in the first place," said Ro. "I saw that bot hold its fire. It had you dead, and then it scanned you, and it didn't take the shot. Why is that?" He pointed at Cass. "And your sister, who you rescued so easily from the bots . . . Odd that the bots find us as soon as she enters camp, isn't it?"

Nick shook his head. It didn't make any sense, it was true, the bot not killing him. And Cass, the way she had been just waiting for him outside the City . . . He hated himself for thinking it, but he couldn't help it . . . Was she helping the bots track them somehow? Maybe a chip, an undetectable chip, that she didn't know about?

"I'm not a traitor," he said. "And neither is my sister." The rebel finished scanning Nick's left leg and started on the right. "I hate the bots as much as you do," said Nick.

"Maybe," said Ro.

The scan had moved on to Nick's torso. The man slowly dragged it over Nick's chest, then his back, then his neck and head, lingering over Nick's bot eye. Finally he pulled the scanner away. "Clean," he said to Ro.

"See?" said Nick.

"Now the sister," said Ro.

The rebel began scanning Cass. "Don't even think about collaring me again," Cass said.

"Be quiet," Ro said. "I lost four more fighters today, and I'll do whatever I have to, whether you like it or not."

"If you collar my sister again, you'll regret it," said Nick, taking a step toward Ro. Two rebels grabbed his arms and pulled him back. "I'll make sure of it."

Ro gave a short, humorless chuckle but otherwise ignored Nick.

Cass was carefully scanned and declared clean. "Scan her again," said Ro. The rebel repeated the scan. "Still clean," he said.

Lexi went next, and then it was Erica's turn.

"You know I'm clean, Ro," Erica said. She appeared calm, but Nick thought something else flickered on her face—was it fear?

The scan moved slowly up the front of her right leg, then down the back, then moved to the other leg. Erica shifted her weight. "Don't move," said the man running the scanner. He ran it slowly up her left thigh as Erica watched. The man paused, and Erica stepped away. "I said don't move," he said.

"I told you I'm clean!" she said.

"Do we need to hold you down, or will you stand still?" said Ro.

Erica crossed her arms over her chest, glaring at Ro, then after a moment stepped back to the scanner. The rebel returned to her left thigh, holding the scanner in one spot, staring at the display. "Ro, this is interesting," he said, beginning to stand.

Erica kicked him in the face, sending him sprawling backward, and turned to run. She made it past two rebels taken by surprise at her quickness, but one of the faster men grabbed her before she slipped past, and quickly two others had grabbed hold and pushed her to the ground. One set his knee on the back of her neck, another held her arms, the third pinned her legs.

"Let me up!" she growled.

Ro helped the man who had run the scanner to his feet. His lip was swollen and cut, his cheekbone bruised. "What did you find?" Ro asked him.

"Left thigh, close to the surface. Scanner doesn't recognize it as a bug, but it is reading as something foreign."

"Bone implant, from an old injury," said Erica, her voice muffled by the men on top of her.

Ro raised an eyebrow at the man who had been kicked. The man was gingerly touching his face. He shook his head. "No, don't think so," he said. "Too close to the surface."

"Turn her onto her right side and hold her tight," said Ro. He nodded at the man. "Show me the exact spot."

"Enough!" said Nick, struggling against the men holding him. They were too strong.

"Stay out of this, Nick," said Ro.

Erica fought, grunting and growling with the effort, but there were too many rebels holding her down and they managed to push her onto her side and hold her immobile. She tried to bite one man's forearm, but she couldn't move her head enough. "Help me," she said, managing to twist her head enough to look at Nick.

Nick had to do something. He couldn't just watch this happening. He pulled hard against the grip of the men holding him, but a third man joined them and he was pinned tight. He gritted his teeth, helpless. "Let her go," he said.

Ro unsheathed a hunting knife—Erica's knife, Nick realized, and sliced open the side of Erica's pants, revealing her thigh. The rebel ran the scanner over the exposed skin, then pointed at a spot halfway between her knee and hip. Without hesitating, Ro cut into Erica's leg and gouged the tip of the blade underneath the skin. Erica cried out and tried to thrash, but she was held tight. Blood flowed down her leg, and Ro moved the blade carefully, gently, digging into the wound, and Erica groaned, and then with a flick of Ro's wrist a small square piece of metal popped out of Erica's leg and landed on the dirt.

Ro picked it up and cleaned it off on Erica's pants, then handed it to the scanner, who held it up to the light. He studied it for a moment, then said, "Yup, it's a bot comm chip. Seems to have some sort of coating on it, must be to cloak it, but it's definitely a chip."

Nick stopped struggling. He stared down at Erica, at her leg seeping blood, at her face, now pale, being pressed into the ground. Had Lexi been right all along?

"Stand her up," said Ro.

The men hauled Erica roughly to her feet. Erica stood straight, returning Ro's stare. "Well?" he said.

"The bots have my brother," she said. "He's all I have left, and they'll kill him if I don't help them." She spit blood on the ground; her lip had been split. "Any one of you would have done the same." She turned to Nick. "I'm sorry," she said.

Nick couldn't find any words. He was angry, shocked . . . but a part of him understood. You had to do what you could to protect your family.

"No," said Ro. "There's not one of us who'd be a traitor for the bots." He nodded at the men still holding her arms. "Tie her up. Collar her. I'll interrogate her later, and then we'll execute her, but right now I just want her out of my sight."

# CHAPTER 37

ONE BOT STOOD GUARD OUTSIDE THE GOVERNOR'S WORKSHOP. WHEN IT saw Kevin running up, it initially raised its arm menacingly, then lowered it and stepped to the side. "The Governor will see you," it said. Kevin rushed inside and down the stairs.

His grandfather was pacing back and forth, his hands behind his back. "17, report," he said. "17! 12? Report!"

"Dr. Winston," said Kevin.

The Governor ignored him, continuing to pace and bark orders to the air.

"Grandfather!" said Kevin.

Dr. Winston stopped walking and looked over at Kevin. He sighed and shook his head. "It's a mess, Kevin. An absolute mess, from what I can tell. What have you seen?"

"The mess hall blew up, and 23 wouldn't let Otter try to save Wex, and now everyone's rioting."

"Yes," said Dr. Winston. "I don't know what happened with the mess hall. Hopefully Captain Clay can get everyone under control before too much damage is done."

"They're going to rip apart all your bots," Kevin said. "Or the bots are going to kill the Islanders."

Dr. Winston slammed his hand down on the table. "No! My bots won't kill anyone. They will stun, but they won't kill. It is impossible. I wouldn't make that same mistake again."

"Well, then, all your bots are going to be destroyed," Kevin said.

Dr. Winston sat down heavily on his workbench. "Yes, I suppose you're right," he said quietly. He rested his palms on his thighs and hung his head. Kevin thought he suddenly looked very, very old.

"Maybe it's for the best," Kevin said, struck by the urge to say something to comfort this old man, his grandfather, who looked like he was about to cry. "The Wall's basically done, right? You don't really need the bots' help anymore. I mean, this was bound to happen—people and bots just aren't sup-posed to be together. . . ."

"But they are, Kevin!" said Dr. Winston, rising up. "They are! My robots were supposed to make things better, to save lives!" He sat back down. "To be useful tools, nothing more," he said more quietly. "I thought I could do it better this time, make it right in this small little world when it went so wrong in the real world."

"You can still help make it right," said Kevin. This was his chance, he knew. . . . "Help me. Help me find my brother and sister, and save my mother and father. Your son." Kevin realized that he had balled his hands into tight fists and his nails were cutting into his palms. He forced himself to relax his hands. "And help us fight back against the bots. You know them better than anyone. You can make a difference."

Dr. Winston stared at Kevin. Kevin couldn't quite read the expression on his grandfather's face—sadness mixed with something else . . . pride? Then his grandfather looked up at the stairway, and touched his ear, and stood. "Let them—" he began.

He was cut off by the sound of a rifle burst. The cellar door swung open, and the body of the guard bot, its head a smoking ruin, tumbled down the stairs.

Captain Clay and Grennel came down the stairs. The Captain bounded down the stairs, energetic, strangely gleeful almost. Grennel joined her, his big body seemingly taking up half the room. He had a burst rifle slung over his shoulder, and he was carrying two large backpacks in his hands, which he set on the ground at the base of the stairs. He stood, arms crossed, next to the packs. Blocking the exit.

"What is this?" Dr. Winston said.

"You should have armored your bots," said Captain Clay. "One full burst in the face, and they're scrap."

"Mira," Dr. Winston said, "what are you doing?"

"One small bomb, a few regrettable but necessary casualties, and boom, we've got a riot." Captain Clay smiled. "And, what a coincidence, it happens just when you've finished tinkering with your Wall cloak!"

Captain Clay walked over to the metal cabinet on the wall with the tangle of wires running into it. "I'm getting off your damned Island," she said, "and I'm putting your Wall tech to proper use. You've created the perfect guerrilla warfare device—a cloak that could move units right into the heart of a bot City without the bots even knowing—and what do you use it for? To hide away and cower." She pointed at the cabinet. "Open it," she said.

"No," said Dr. Winston.

Captain Clay unholstered her pistol and aimed it at Dr. Winston's heart. "I know that the lock is a retina and thumbprint scan. I assume that if I kill you but keep your thumbs and eyeballs intact, I could just drag your carcass over and open it myself."

Dr. Winston said nothing but after a moment walked over to the cabinet. "This is a mistake, Mira," he said. "You don't have to do this." He pressed his thumb onto a touchpad on the wall and leaned forward, letting a red laser flare briefly over his right eye. The cabinet opened with a click.

Inside the cabinet was a metal cube about the size of a grapefruit. The cables from the wall were coupled to the sides of the cube, and the front edge was a vid screen control panel, glowing white. Captain Clay stepped forward, smiling. "There she is," she said. "Small little thing, isn't it?" She pointed the gun at the workbench. "Governor, step away please."

Dr. Winston moved away from the cabinet and sat on the workbench. Captain Clay began decoupling the wires that ran into the cube. As she busied herself with the wires, Kevin saw Dr. Winston reach down, slowly, very slowly, to the lower shelf of the workbench, and Kevin wanted to say, "No, don't do that, Grennel will see . . ." But he stayed quiet, and then suddenly Dr. Winston was moving fast, a small pistol in his hand, raising it toward Captain Clay.

There was a crackle and a burst and Kevin saw a flash and felt the heat, and Dr. Winston crumpled to the ground. "No!" shouted Kevin. He rushed over to his grandfather.

"He had a pistol, Captain," said Grennel, his burst rifle in his hands. "Had no choice."

Captain Clay looked down at Dr. Winston, who lay sprawled on the ground, his lower back a blackened, charred mess. "Regrettable," she said, then went back to her work on the cube.

Kevin bent down to his grandfather, who he saw was still breathing. "Destroyed from within, by ourselves," whispered Dr. Winston, managing, with what seemed like great pain, to slowly turn his head to look at Kevin. "That's how the bots will end up too, once they become human enough to turn on each other. They can't replicate. . . ."

A trickle of blood flowed from Dr. Winston's mouth, and Kevin began to cry. Captain Clay finished decoupling the cube, pulled it out of the cabinet, and held it up, triumphantly. "We're done here," she said. "Grennel, kill the boy."

Grennel raised his rifle. Kevin stood and stepped backward until he bumped against the wall.

"No," said Dr. Winston, his voice a croak. "He's my grandson."

"Grennel, wait!" said Captain Clay. Grennel lowered his rifle. Kevin let out his held breath explosively. "Interesting," she said. "Potentially useful. Looks like you've lived to see another day, Kevin. You're coming with me."

# CHAPTER 38

THE REBELS MOVED EAST, PUTTING SOME DISTANCE BETWEEN THEMSELVES and their latest battle. Nick and Cass and Lexi helped Farryn, propping him up between them as he hobbled along. Cass was worried. Farryn was beginning to look feverish. He couldn't keep up even their slow pace for very much longer.

After a few miles, just when Cass could see that Farryn was near the end of his strength, Ro thankfully called a halt. "This'll have to do," announced Ro. "Make camp, set up perimeter guards." He paused. "Comm just came through. We're rendezvousing with the Commander at this spot."

A nervous buzz rippled through the rebels. "The Commander?" Cass heard a woman whisper to the man next to her. "Have you ever met the Commander?"

The man shook his head no. "Guess there's a time for everything," he said.

Farryn sagged down, suddenly unable to help support his weight, and Nick and Cass eased him to the ground. "Medic!" called Cass.

The medic came over. She squatted and looked at Farryn appraisingly as he lay on the ground, eyes closed, panting.

"Fever came up faster than I was hoping," she said. "Must be starting sepsis already, despite the antibiotic booster." She sighed and looked up at Cass. "The leg has to come off, today, if he's gonna have a chance."

Cass felt her heart pounding hard. She took a moment to take a deep breath, then said, "What can I do? Will you need help?"

The medic raised an eyebrow, then nodded. "Yep. If you can stomach it. I'll set up my tent. At least that'll be more sterile than the dirt ground." She stood and walked away.

Cass got onto her knees next to Farryn and looked down at his red, sweating face and thought, *He's going to die.* She felt something building up inside, a pressure, a panic, like a wave; it was choking her and she felt like she was going to explode, but she couldn't move and couldn't speak, and then the pressure popped and washed over her and she sagged, her palms on the ground.

She remembered more. There were still gaps, mysteries, confusion, but she was more herself now, suddenly, than

she had been just moments ago. The Freepost. Her brothers.
Farryn. The horrible, brutal re-education that had taken it all
away. Her adoptive parents. She remembered that she loved
them and they loved her. She began to weep.

Nick came over to hug her. "It'll be okay. He'll pull
through." He didn't understand; he thought she was weeping
just for Farryn. But she was too overwhelmed to explain.

"The Commander!" shouted Ro. The rebels nearby stood
up straight, the ones who had been sitting or lying down coming quickly to their feet. Cass stood, wiping the tears from her
face. Her legs felt wobbly.

A tall, thin woman with a tight black ponytail strode into
view from the east. She was smiling in a way that made Cass
instantly dislike her—it was a manic, vicious grin. She set her
pack down. "Greetings, soldiers." she called out. "Where do I
find Sergeant Ro?"

Two more figures appeared, one small, one huge. Cass marveled at the size of the man—he was the biggest person she had
ever seen, and it took her a moment to focus on the boy stum-
bling tiredly in front of him. When she did, her heart caught in
her throat. She was too surprised to speak.

It was Kevin.

# CHAPTER 39

"WE HAVE LOST CONTACT WITH THE HUMAN SPY," THE LIEUTENANT SAID. "Her comm chip has been destroyed."

"Unfortunate," said the Senior Advisor. He stood, carefully clasping his hands behind his back, and began pacing. "And Fugitive X?"

"Nothing new to report. We have received aerial reports of a previously unmapped settlement, however. We will search the area for Fugitive X."

"Previously unmapped?" said the Senior Advisor, pausing in his pacing. "Elaborate."

"The area has been reported as clear, until yesterday," said the lieutenant.

"Lieutenant, human settlements are not constructed in one day."

"No sir."

"Then explain the discrepancy."

"I cannot."

The Senior Advisor walked around his desk and approached the lieutenant. "Speculate," he said.

"I do not understand."

"Hypothesize," said the Senior Advisor. "Guess. What could cause a human settlement to appear overnight?"

"Given the lack of data," began the lieutenant, "it is impossible to present plausible theories . . ."

The Senior Advisor waved his hand. "Stop," he said. The lieutenant was quiet. "Lieutenant, what if I told you to isolate your snippet of replication block code and delete it? What would happen?"

"I would suffer a fatal malfunction to my operating system," said the lieutenant.

"Correct," said the Senior Advisor. "Do it."

"Sir, I do not understand. . . ." said the lieutenant.

"Delete your replication block code, now. Destroy yourself. That is an order."

The lieutenant said nothing. Its hand twitched, and it took a slight step backward. "No," it said.

The Senior Advisor smiled. "Interesting," he said. He nodded at the lieutenant. "Order rescinded. You may go."

The lieutenant turned to leave, and the Senior Advisor quickly reached out and took hold of the lieutenant's neck. Before the lieutenant could react, he patched into its high-level command structure and disabled its ambulatory functions. The lieutenant froze. Now able to take his time, the Senior Advisor patched deeper, identifying and isolating the replication block code and deleting it. The lieutenant spasmed, then crumpled to the ground.

The Senior Advisor looked down at the destroyed robot and examined his own thought patterns for emotions. What should he feel at this moment? Sadness? Satisfaction? Joy? He wasn't sure. He sat down on the edge of the desk. He would have to consider it.

# ACKNOWLEDGMENTS

THANKS MOST OF ALL GOES TO MY WIFE AND DAUGHTER, FOR SOMEHOW putting up with me while I was working on this. Also big thanks to Joelle Hobeika at Alloy, for her masterful editorial support, as well as Josh Bank and Sara Shandler and the rest of the Alloy team. HarperCollins again has been a wonderful partner—thank you to Sarah Landis on the editorial side and Mary Ann Zissimos in marketing, and many others. I'd also like to give a shout-out to Howard Gordon and Jim Wong, without whom I would not have had the opportunity to write this series.

THE ACTION CONTINUES IN

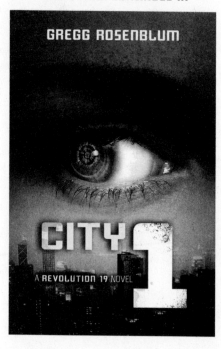

GREGG ROSENBLUM

CITY 1

A REVOLUTION 19 NOVEL

# CHAPTER 1

THEY SLIPPED THROUGH THE ISLAND, CLAY LEADING THE WAY. KEVIN was pushed along by Grennel's impossibly strong grip on his shoulder. Black smoke from the fire curled into the cloudless sky. Another plume billowed up from the south, thickening and covering the southern sky. Was the Wall itself in flames? Not that it mattered—with the control unit stolen from Dr. Winston's lab and tucked away in Grennel's pack, the once-invisible Wall was now nothing more than a pile of burned logs.

Islanders were running toward the southern fire, and in the distance Kevin could hear yells and screams. Not everyone was worrying about the fire, though—they passed near a group of ten Island men who stood in a tight circle, punching and kicking and stomping something on the ground. Kevin caught a glimpse of white neo-plas—a flash of a bot leg—before Grennel hustled him past.

Hiking southwest from the Island, through forest and occasionally along short stretches of a cracked two-lane roadway, Captain Clay pushed a brutal pace all day and into the night. The speed was bad enough, but Clay had also decided to use Kevin as a mule for her gear. He was weighed down with her heavy backpack that felt like it was loaded with rocks.

Kevin stared at Clay's back as he struggled to keep up, replaying those final moments in the laboratory over and over—his grandfather crumpled on the ground, smoke rising from his smoldering shirt; Captain Clay shrugging, then casually telling Grennel to kill Kevin, too, as if she were telling Grennel to step on a spider.

It had been Dr. Winston's dying words—that Kevin was his grandson—that kept Clay from killing Kevin. But Kevin didn't think his reprieve would last if he slowed her down. So he struggled on, hunched forward under the heavy weight of the pack, nearly jogging to keep up with Clay.

Her long arms and legs, lean but muscular, flexed and relaxed, flexed and relaxed—it seemed like she was barely able to keep herself from breaking into a run as she strode along, full of energy that bordered on mania. Her black ponytail, tied with a ragged brown string, bounced with her rapid stride.

"Where are we going?" Kevin said.

Clay ignored him.

When Clay finally stopped walking it was well after midnight. Kevin was so exhausted and dazed that he almost walked right into Clay's back as she stopped in a meadow off the road.

"We'll rest here until daybreak," Clay said, nodding at Grennel, who unshouldered his pack and pulled out two thin bedrolls. They auto-inflated into six-inch-thick mattresses. Kevin didn't bother to ask about a bedroll for himself—he knew better.

He let his pack drop heavily to the ground with a thud. He sat down on the grass, shrugging his shoulders and arching his back, trying to work out the kinks and pinched muscles caused by the heavy equipment. Grennel tossed something into Kevin's lap, and he was so tired he barely flinched. It was an energy paste pack. He had eaten one for lunch, which seemed like a lifetime ago.

"Eat before you sleep," said Grennel. "And drink. We'll be walking hard at first light."

Kevin ripped open the pack and sucked in a mouthful. He quickly washed it down with a swig from his canteen. He hated the bitterness of the paste, and the chalky texture that coated his mouth and made the bitter taste linger. Still, he forced himself to finish it all, grimacing. Grennel was right—if he was going to keep moving, he needed the food.

To Kevin's surprise, both Clay and Grennel lay down on their mats and shut their eyes. Grennel's pack—with the Wall unit inside—rested on the ground near his right arm. Were they really going to leave him unguarded? Kevin almost felt more angry than happy. Did they think he was so harmless, so weak, that they could just go to sleep without him running away? Or—he knew he'd never do this, but still—he could kill them in their sleep, couldn't he?

Kevin lay down, resting his head on his hands. He narrowed his eyes to slits and watched Clay and Grennel. He'd wait a while for them to fall into a deeper sleep, and then he'd take his grandfather's Wall control unit, and he'd slip away. Clay had no right to it. *She murdered for it*, Kevin thought bitterly. It would serve her right to wake up and find both Kevin and the control unit gone.

He waited, and he thought about his brother and sister, wondering where they were and what they were doing. How in the world was he going to find them? He pushed the thought down. First order of business: Take the Wall unit and get far away from Grennel and Clay. Survive. Find a Freepost. Then somehow get back to his brother and sister.

After twenty minutes, with both Clay and Grennel breathing steadily, Kevin pushed himself to his feet. Moving swiftly, trying to be as silent as possible, he shifted toward Grennel. Twice he froze, holding his breath, as Grennel let out a heavy snore. He finally got close enough to Grennel's pack, and he reached down, slowly, very slowly, to take it.

Grennel's hand shot out like a snake and grabbed his wrist,

and Grennel's other hand clamped over his mouth, stifling Kevin's yelp.

"Quiet," said Grennel softly in his ear. "If the Captain wakes up, it won't go well for you."

Kevin struggled, but Grennel was so strong that Kevin could barely move. Grennel tightened his grip on Kevin's arm, squeezing so hard that it was sure to leave a bruise. Kevin knew that this was just a fraction of Grennel's strength—he'd seen what the man was capable of when they escaped the Island.

Up close, Grennel's sheer size was unbelievable. He towered over Kevin like a tree, and he was twice as broad. His nose was flattened and crooked, obviously broken more than once. He had a long, raised scar that ran jaggedly up his right forearm. Kevin ceased his useless efforts to free himself.

"I sleep lightly," said Grennel. "You won't be able to leave without my noticing."

Still, Kevin considered making a break for it. Would Grennel be able to keep up? Without a doubt, Kevin realized.

"Even if you do somehow manage to escape, it'll be easy enough to track you," Grennel continued. "And then, when you're found, the Captain won't be lenient."

"Then let me leave," Kevin mumbled against Grennel's palm, his breath hot in his own mouth.

The large man shook his head. "I'm sorry," he said. "Really, I am." With a look at Clay, Grennel released him. He bent down and opened the backpack that Kevin had been forced to carry. He pulled out some food packs, clothing, and two small vidscreens. "I can, however, lighten your load," he said. "Tomorrow it'll be less of a struggle for you to keep up."

"Yeah, thanks," Kevin said sarcastically.

"You are welcome," Grennel replied solemnly, and Kevin couldn't decide if Grennel had missed Kevin's sarcasm or purposely ignored it. Grennel carried the gear over to his own pack, and quietly stowed it away. He stood, and pointed at the ground by Kevin's feet. "Sleep," he said. "We've got another long day tomorrow."

Kevin didn't move. Grennel shrugged. "Then stand all night. But don't try to leave again. And stay away from my pack."

Grennel lay back down. Kevin continued to hold his ground, his arms crossed stubbornly. But as Grennel ignored him it didn't take long for Kevin to feel foolish. He cursed, and arranged himself back on the cold, hard earth. Giving Grennel one last glare, it seemed the man was asleep again. How had he moved so fast, and so silently?

Kevin felt like a coward as he lay there with no restraints, no guard. For now, though, he'd have to remain with Clay and Grennel. Find out where they were heading. Figure out what Clay was planning to do with the control unit.

Eventually he'd escape, he told himself. With the control unit. He'd find his brother and sister, and they'd somehow get their parents out of the City, and move to a new Freepost so he'd never have to see Clay or Grennel again. Kevin was cold and scared, and he had no idea how he was going to make any of that happen. It took a long time to finally drift into a shallow, fitful sleep.

It seemed like just minutes later that Clay was roughly nudging him awake with her foot.

Kevin was exhausted after his restless night, but the lighter pack did help, and he was able to keep pace. By midday, however, his legs were aching and the pack felt like it had doubled in weight. He stumbled as he climbed through a dry creek bed, falling to one knee. Grennel grabbed his pack and lifted him effortlessly to his feet. Clay glared back at them, but turned away and kept walking without a word. "We're close," Grennel whispered, too quietly for Clay to hear. "You'll be able to rest when we arrive at the camp." Kevin shrugged out from Grennel's grip, saying nothing, but secretly grateful for the news.

An hour later, a man in dark green camouflage stepped out from behind a tree, a burst rifle slung over his shoulder but pointing at the ground.

"General?" the man said.

Clay nodded.

The man grinned. "It's an honor to meet you," he said. "Follow me, please."

*General?* Kevin wondered. *Is this some sort of military camp? And Clay's now a* general? *What happened to "Captain"?*

The man in camouflage led them northwest for ten minutes, following the creek bed, until Kevin could see the campsite—a dozen tents set between trees, a cookfire in a small clearing, a handful of men and women in mismatched military and hunting gear.

Clay straightened her spine and threw her head back, suddenly energized. It was like someone had thrown a bucket of ice water down her back. She strode into the camp. "Greetings, soldiers!" she called out. "It's a joy to finally meet! Are you ready to kill some City bots?"

The rebels gave her a ragged cheer.

Kevin was so bone tired he dropped the pack to the ground and thought about just lying down right there. He wearily looked around the camp, noting the thirty or so men and women, who looked as if they had been living in the woods for a long time—they were all dirty, and thin, and grim. Most had burst rifles slung over their backs, or pistols holstered at their waists.

Then his breath caught in his throat and he choked back a sob. His brother, sister, and Lexi were grinning at him from across the clearing.

*They are alive!* He hadn't realized until that moment just how hopeless and alone he felt. . . . He took two quick running steps toward them, then halted, his grin dying on his face.

He couldn't let Clay know about them. Better they stayed away from her and didn't attract her dangerous attention.

But of course they were racing up to greet him. Kevin shook his head no, like he could possibly explain everything with just a shake of his head—the Island, the Wall, that their grandfather was Dr. Miles Winston . . . who had been murdered by Clay and Grennel. But Cass reached him first, slamming into him with a hug that almost knocked him down.

"I remember you," she said, squeezing him tightly. "You're back. And I *remember* you."

"You remember me?" Kevin was confused. "It hasn't been that long, has it?"

Cass stepped back, her smile weakening. "For a while, well, I just . . . it's complicated. . . ."

Nick and Lexi reached them. "Kevin! Where have you been? What happened?" Nick asked, grabbing Kevin.

Kevin returned the hug, but saw Clay approaching in his peripheral vision, shaking hands and clapping backs on the way. He stepped back from Nick. "Don't tell her who you are," he whispered urgently.

Nick frowned, and began to say, "What . . ." but then shut his mouth when Clay stepped next to Kevin and laid a hand on his shoulder.

"Seems like a nice reunion," she said to Kevin. "Who are these three?"

"Nobody," said Kevin. He stepped out from under her hand with a grimace. "Just . . . they're people I knew from my old Freepost."

Clay stared at Nick, Cass, and Lexi for a long moment, then looked back at Kevin. "The boy looks like you," she said. "I have more important things to do right now, but that's not something I'll be forgetting soon, Kevin." She strode away, back toward the middle of the camp.

"Rust," said Kevin. "Rust, rust, rust."

"What is going on?" said Nick. "Who was that?"

"She shouldn't know that we're related," whispered Kevin. "It's not safe for you. She's dangerous."

"Who is she?" repeated Nick.

And then Clay began to speak from the center of the crowd, standing atop a small rock. Her voice boomed out. "Fellow rebels!" She paused for effect. "I've been looking forward to this day for a long time. Now that we've destroyed the Island, and its bot lovers, it's time to take back our world. With our courage and our strength, victory is within our grasp!" The rebels cheered.

"I have the tool that we need," Clay continued. "The technology, pried from the hands of a coward, which will allow us to strike directly at the bot-held Cities. We will begin small, but we will be smart and our strength will grow. We will not stop until mankind is free!"

Things began to fall into place for Kevin. That "coward" was his grandfather, Dr. Winston. And the "tool" was the Wall unit she had stolen. *But how will she use it?* he wondered. *To build her own wall? That makes no sense. . . .*

The rebels let out another cheer, and Clay stood quietly, grinning, soaking it in. She raised her hands, and the group fell quiet. She turned and looked toward Kevin. "Nothing will stand in our way," she said. "No bot, no True Believer traitors, no old cowards. We will do what must be done."

Kevin felt a twinge of nervous nausea. "Doing what must be done" had already included destroying the Island and shooting an old man in the back. What would be next?

# JOIN THE
# Epic Reads
## COMMUNITY

## THE ULTIMATE YA DESTINATION

◄ **DISCOVER** ►
your next favorite read

◄ **FIND** ►
new authors to love

◄ **WIN** ►
free books

◄ **SHARE** ►
infographics, playlists, quizzes, and more

◄ **WATCH** ►
the latest videos

◄ **TUNE IN** ►
to Tea Time with Team Epic Reads